To

John & Juawn

THE ADVENTURES OF GINGER BREAD WILLIE

Best Wishes

D.L. Blake

9/3/12

THE ADVENTURES OF GINGER BREAD WILLIE

DEBORAH L. BLAKE

authorHOUSE®

AuthorHouse™
1663 Liberty Drive
Bloomington, IN 47403
www.authorhouse.com
Phone: 1-800-839-8640

First published by AuthorHouse   10/14/2011

ISBN: 978-1-4567-9722-5 (sc)
ISBN: 978-1-4567-9723-2 (ebk)

Printed in the United States of America

Any people depicted in stock imagery provided by Thinkstock are models, and such images are being used for illustrative purposes only.

Certain stock imagery © Thinkstock.

This book is printed on acid-free paper.

CHAPTER ONE

Isn't it weird that everything has to make sense or we don't understand it. Well with a little creativity and some fun anything can happen, so all I ask is forget what is normal and enjoy my imagination, nothing is impossible.

Ginger Bread Willie is a character who was created quite accidentally one day when Ma Louise Cahill was mixing up her usual gingerbread dough in the kitchen of her little house in Arizona. The telephone rang and she went to answer leaving the mixture in the basin. While she was chatting on the telephone her ten year old Grandson who was visiting from Phoenix went into the kitchen to look for something to eat.

The air was filled with flour from baking and the young boy breathed it up his nose. He felt a tickle in his nose and wiggled his nose to try and get rid of it. The tickle did not go away, he rubbed his nose with the back of his hand, and the tickle still didn't go away. Suddenly he let out a full blown sneeze without having time to cover his mouth and nose, he turned his head to the side as he sneezed, droplets landed in the gingerbread mixture. The little boy tried to wipe off the droplets with his hands but it spread.

He had been playing in a hot spring that day and his sleeves were wet so he gently rubbed the damp sleeves over the gingerbread mixture to see if that would wipe away the droplets. It didn't look too bad and he was sure that the heat in the oven would kill any germs. He grabbed a piece of bread and went back into the garden.

Ma Cahill finished on the telephone and went into the kitchen; she decided she would make three large gingerbread people today because she wanted to put them outside and use them as an advertisement so customers could find her from the main road. She was famous for her cakes and biscuits and that was how she earned her living.

She rolled out the mixture and hand crafted a lovely gingerbread man and two gingerbread women with great concentration and precision. They were about two feet tall. She brushed them with egg yolk, put them on a baking sheet and placed them in the oven. She made herself a cup of coffee and sat and waited for the gingerbread people to cook. After twenty minutes they were a lovely golden colour and cooked to perfection, she lifted the tray out of the oven and put it to one side to cool.

Ma Cahill looked through her cupboard to see what she could use for their eyes and other features. She decided to use food colouring so they would look more original and full of character. She started with one of the gingerbread women, she painted a pair of brown bunches on her head, cute little freckles on her face and dainty little features. She looked very pretty, Ma Cahill decided that this little lady should be a bit of a cowgirl, so painted dungarees on her and a checked shirt; she painted some cowgirl boots on her feet and named her Gingerbread Jane.

The second lady was going to be a Harvey girl who served at El Tovar Hotel, Grand Canyon Village on the south rim. She was given a black full length dress with a starched white apron and a white bow in her hair. Strangely no matter how hard Ma Cahill tried she could not seem to paint a nice friendly face on this one. She named her Gingerbread Fanny.

Now for the gingerbread man, Ma Cahill was not sure what she wanted to do with him so she looked around the house for some inspiration. She went into her bedroom and in her trunk, under her moonshine stash, she found a picture of her Grandfather William Cahill. He was very handsome and an old fashioned cowboy, that was the perfect look for her gingerbread man and he would be named after her Grandfather to become Gingerbread Willie. She created a cute cowboy outfit for him with awesome boots which were tough enough to keep rattle snakes from biting his legs and feet, and gave him the sweetest little face she could. He was a very happy smiley little guy. She sat them in the hammock on the porch.

That evening Ma Cahill was lonely, she sat on her porch wishing her moonshine making partner Skippity Jack Moran was there so she had someone to sit with and get totally wasted on moonshine and suck away on pickled eggs. She decided there was no point sitting and feeling sorry for herself she should get some varnish and paint her gingerbread people to prevent them from becoming wet, damaged or decaying. She went to look for the varnish leaving them on the porch.

While she was gone, a very strange and sinister looking character who had been watching her from behind a bush moved towards the gingerbread people, he was looking for food and could smell them. He had a very drawn and lived in appearance, his clothes were dirty and torn and he looked as though he had not eaten or washed in months. He moved forward, the smell of the gingerbreads beckoning him. As he drew closer, he reached out his hand and took hold of Fanny in his sweaty grubby hands.

At that moment, Ma Cahill returned with her pot of varnish, she spotted the stranger and yelled at him to put her Fanny down. He immediately did so. He apologised to Ma Cahill and told her he had not eaten in days. She felt sorry for him and told him to stay on the porch and she would fix him something to eat.

She went into the house took some bread, cheese and fruit from the kitchen and she found an old thermos flask which she filled with coffee. She returned outside and gave it to the man. He thanked her, she told him that she was expecting the Sheriff soon, this made the man nervous, he took the food and the flask and left.

He walked away from the house in the direction of the Canyon, he turned once as he walked away and the glint in his eyes made Ma Cahill shiver all over. She had a gut feeling that this man was a bad one. She had lied when she told the man the Sheriff was on the way because she wanted him to leave, and the feeling she had in her gut told her to telephone the Sheriff anyway and report his visit. She rang the local station and was told the sheriff was on his way.

Sheriff Earl was on duty, he told her to make sure she locked all her windows and doors and he would patrol the area around her house at various times during the night. He explained there was a wanted fugitive in the area and he may have been the one she had encountered. He told her not to worry because he would be close by if she needed him. She told him she had to go out to take a parcel to the post office, he took the parcel for her and said he would deal with it she should stay inside and keep safe.

To keep her mind busy and distract her from the fugitive, she turned her attention back to the gingerbreads and began to paint them with the varnish. She talked to them while she brushed them, and told them stories of the Canyon. When they were finished, she placed them on the hammock on the porch to dry and continued to tell them about the wonderful place where they lived.

Soon she became tired and decided to go to bed. She left the gingerbread people on the porch to dry through the night. When she got into her little house Ma Cahill made sure all the windows and doors were closed and locked.

That night there was a full moon and it looked magical against the red sandstone of the plateau, the air was dry and sound travelled for miles across the desert, Ma Cahill snored, broke wind and slept like a baby, she felt safe knowing Sheriff Earl was patrolling the area.

During the night however, it seemed that the magic of the full moon had triggered some other unusual events and something very strange started to happen. Very slowly the three gingerbread people started to come to life, the reason for this was really quite simple.

The child had sneezed leaving his DNA in the dough mixture, it was only a small amount, but it was enough to be a primer. The process which then happened mimicked a scientific process. The mixture had been mixed together quite rapidly with a wooden spoon, and contaminated with bacterial enzymes which the boy picked up from the hot spring which he had been playing in.

These certain bacterial enzymes are not affected by high temperatures and are commonly used to unwind the strands of DNA so that they can copy themselves in a laboratory environment. So with the hot oven temperature and the cooling when they came out of the oven, Ma Cahill had unknowingly provided the exact conditions to allow the process of Polymerase Chain Reaction (PCR), which is the process used to increase the volume of Mitochondrial DNA when a sample is too small to work with. It is in fact just like photocopying a DNA sequence to create more copies.

This meant that this gingerbread family had a human DNA sequence in them, which meant that they were part human which meant that they were technically alive. They had human senses and were capable of human intelligence.

The next morning Ma Cahill went out to her porch to see if her gingerbread family had dried, they were gone.

She was very upset and searched all over the porch and the garden for them. Suddenly she heard the radio playing and the kettle boiling, she ran inside the house and on the sofa sat Gingerbread Wille and Gingerbread Jane. She looked into the kitchen, and Gingerbread Fanny was making coffee.

"Who the hell are you and what are you doing in my house" she screamed

Willie ran up to her and said

"Mother its ok it's us"

Ma Cahill reached over to the cushion on the sofa and removed a bottle of moonshine from behind it, she checked the label and said

"What the hell has he given me to drink; he swore to me there was no methanol in this"

She ran out of the house screaming she was so freaked out she didn't know where to go. She ran to the barn and hid behind the mules. Luckily in the barn she had some moonshine stashed under the hay along with some dope. She rolled herself a joint pulled the cork out of the bottle with her teeth and as quick as she could, sucked in the dope and drank down the contents of the bottle.

What the hell was that? What had she just seen? She realised that now she was pissed and high there was less chance of her making sense of what was in her house, in fact when she stood up to peep through the door she realised that walking to the house would be a challenge in itself.

She sat on the floor swearing, she had a very good selection of words which she used in stressful situations and at that moment she recalled and used every one of them. She couldn't call the Sheriff because she didn't have a phone in the barn and how the hell would she explain seeing three two foot tall gingerbread people in her house making themselves coffee and watching television. She really had to think this through. She realised she had to sober up and think of a plan.

Just as she was sitting in the barn going out of her mind, she could hear a voice.

"Ma Cahill, it's Gingerbread Jane, please don't be frightened we are not going to hurt you we are afraid and confused too, we don't know why we are here"

She shouted for Jane to go away she thought it must be a nightmare. Jane walked into the barn and started to cry, she was terrified. The three of them had no concept of what they were or how they came to be, Ma Cahill realised she was going to have to face this and sort it out. She told Jane to sit next to her and they would try and figure out what the hell had happened. Jane was sobbing and that made her more afraid because she didn't know what human emotions were and why she was doing it.

Ma Cahill gave Jane a cuddle, she realised that whatever had happened was a complete freak of nature but it could also be a blessing. She stood up and although a bit wobbly managed to walk to the house with Jane.

Willie was still sitting on the sofa he was picking at his varnish trying to work out what the hell he was. Fanny was in the kitchen and was playing with a batch of gingerbread people which Ma Cahill had put aside for a customer. She looked puzzled as to why they were not walking and talking like her, Jane and Willie. That really was a good question wasn't it.

Ma Cahill knew something had happened with this batch of dough, which had not happened to any other but what the hell was it? She remembered about her Grandson the day before and wondered if there was a connection between his visit and the Gingerbreads coming to life. Maybe the child had a little go at mixing the dough and made a wish kids were always doing things like that.

Ginger Bread Jane

She telephoned her son in Phoenix and asked if she could speak to her Grandson Michael she explained to the child that he was not in trouble, but Grandma needed to know if he had done anything to the dough when he was in the kitchen. He was very quiet and didn't want to admit to sneezing in the dough. She explained to him that the dough was not going to be eaten so if something had happened it wasn't a problem.

He told his Grandma exactly what had happened to the dough, including the part when he had tried to wipe it with his sleeves which had been wet from the spring, she didn't know what this meant but it must have had something to do with Michael and his sneeze.

If she approached someone else about this she would be locked up for sure but how would she figure out what happened. She sat and thought about that sneeze, she did have a slight interest in DNA as she liked to watch crime programmes on the television.

She got onto the internet and searched for DNA, she looked through the different types and then she read about a case where the body of a person needed to be identified but almost all of his body had been eaten by a crocodile. Only a small piece of DNA was available to work with. The sample went through a process called Polymerase Chain Reaction to increase it so it could be tested.

The article described the conditions which were needed for the PCR technique, and When Ma Cahill sat and thought through the process the dough would have gone through that day she realised that the mixing, heat and cooling with the addition of the sneeze and the bacteria from the spring had created life.

She went into the kitchen and made some coffee, then she sat the three gingerbreads down on the sofa and explained to them what she believed had happened. They sat and listened but it was a little too much for their limited knowledge to take in so Ma Cahill gave each of them a hug and told them that they had been blessed with the gift of life and that she would love them and take care of them the best she could.

She felt a great deal of responsibility, and was determined to do her best for them. She got up from her seat and hurried around the house finding every book she owned, she found pens, paper, and an abacus, and then set up a classroom on the porch. She would school them.

During the days and evenings she taught them everything she knew and what she didn't know she read to them from books. While educating them they began to show how different they were in personality and strengths.

Fanny was a very bossy girl; she was excellent at cooking and spent all the spare time she had in the kitchen creating wonderful dishes and desserts. She was very strong willed and could sometimes be very overbearing. She was also very determined to get what she wanted. It was difficult for Ma Cahill to get close to her there was something not quite right about Fanny but she couldn't quite put her finger on what it was.

Jane was very pleasant natured, she would sit and listen to country music for hours; she loved to play the banjo which she had learned very quickly. She was very sweet to Ma Cahill and learned how to use a lasso with uncanny precision. Her personality was very timid and she was very emotional but she also had a strong sense of values and would stand up for what she thought was right.

Wille had itchy feet, and a thirst for adventure, although he was always interested in the stories Ma Cahill told his mind would wander off on an adventure. He had a natural sense of survival, possessing it as a sixth sense it was so sharp. He was fascinated by the Canyon and the explorers who had been there especially one armed Major John Wesley Powell, who had mapped the then unknown depths of the Canyon on his trip down the Colorado River in 1869. Willie loved books, and watching documentaries he wanted to know as much as he could about the natural world and what inhabited it. He just wanted to be let loose on the planet.

They were all different but the one thing they did have in common was their human DNA, which was the thing which gave them the human qualities which they needed to survive. The most important of those would be instinct.

The rate at which they learnt was truly remarkable, they seemed to thrive on information; they read every book which was put in front of them. One day there were no books left in the house which they hadn't read, so Ma told them she would take them to the library in Flagstaff, she could also pick up some supplies while she was there.

The trip would take at least four hours and they were to travel by mule. Ma Cahill went on a mule named Jacob and the three Gingerbread people rode on a mule named Fig.

The mules were used to walking long distances and usually walked up and down the Canyon on the trails. They packed some food and water to take with them, tied it to the mules and headed for Flagstaff. It was a very hot day and the road was dusty, the heat and the motion of the mule made Fanny fall asleep. Jane played the banjo for them along the way, and Willie sang his heart out.

When they arrived at Flagstaff they headed straight for the library while Ma Cahill went to the trading post to get her supplies. They only had an hour to get what they needed it was another four hour journey back to their Grand Canyon home and they didn't want to be riding the mules in the dark.

The Gingerbread family borrowed as many books as they could and packed them onto the mules. Ma Cahill filled two large bags full of cooking supplies and they were sealed up by the store keeper and he helped her to strap them onto her mule. People couldn't help but stare at the unusual family, but they put the strange sight down to the amount of bootleg moonshine which they washed down on a daily basis.

The mules made their way back onto the path leading back to the Canyon they knew the way and didn't have to be shown. Ma Cahill told the Gingerbreads she wanted to introduce them to some very good friends of hers on the Indian Reservation on the way home.

Very soon they reached the Reservation, Ma Cahill tied up the mules and told the Gingerbreads to follow her. They arrived at a huge campfire which was surrounded by Navajo Indians. They were overjoyed to see her and greeted her with great warmth, she introduced the Gingerbreads to the Navajo and they were very welcoming.

They sat around the campfire and ate boiled mutton and tortillas. When they had finished eating, the Indians danced around the fire and encouraged the Gingerbreads to join in. Ma Cahill thanked the Indians for their hospitality, but explained that they had to continue with their journey home.

Willie was fascinated with the tribe, they said he was welcome to visit at anytime and would show him the art of tracking. Fanny was put out because she could not do any of the cooking, but Jane had a lovely time riding the horses at the reservation. They climbed back onto the mules and made their way home.

Ma Cahill was in desperate need of some moonshine, she had the shakes. When they arrived home they were exhausted but had a wonderful day, the only one who was not very happy was Fanny because she was very saddle sore.

CHAPTER TWO

As morning broke over the Canyon the warm breeze brought lots of curious sounds which echoed around Ma Cahill's little house, sounds of nature which were easily recognisable to the accustomed ear but not to the ears of Gingerbread Willie, all of these sounds were new to him. The freshness and animation of the morning slowly woke him and he opened his eyes. Immediately the happy little guy smiled, he felt so good, what was it that made him feel so happy and cheerful he wondered, then he realised it was the gift of life itself which made him feel like this, but most of all it was his thirst for adventure.

As he sat on his bed looking out of the window, he decided that today was the day he was going to start planning his first adventure. He went into the kitchen where Ma Cahill and Fanny were cooking breakfast and told them that he felt ready to leave the house and start exploring; he was going to start with the Canyon and follow the route which Major Powell took in 1869.

Ma Cahill was sad that Willie was going to be leaving, but she was very proud of him and knew that she had prepared him well for the world. Fanny would be off to her job at The El Tovar Hotel in a couple of days and Jane had been offered a job looking after horses at the Navajo reservation, where they liked her gentle nature. This made Ma Cahill very happy because she would still have Jane home with her when she was not at work.

Willie needed to plan his trip with precision he was going to be the first gingerbread person to navigate his way through the 277 miles of the Colorado River through the Grand Canyon Arizona. He had to be sure he had everything he needed for his trip, and was fully prepared for any circumstance which came his way.

Willie was armed with a book which told him all about the Major Powell expedition, and he was going to recreate his journey as close to it as nature would allow. The only difference was that he wasn't going to start as far away as Major Powell had done, because he sensibly realised that his first lone adventure should be as close to home as possible, but he was determined to ride the rapids and follow the Colorado as best he could. Jane told Willie she would try and join him during his expedition so he had some company, she would wait until he was just below the Grand Canyon Village.

Willie built a raft out of wooden logs which he scrounged from local people, when they learned of his forthcoming adventure they were very interested and he was given lots of things which they thought he may need. Ma Cahill told Willie that he would need to learn some basic cooking skills and spent a day with him in the kitchen baking cowboy biscuits and pancakes, she packed a box full of supplies and ingredients he would need to cook his meals and containers full of coffee. She also gave him several bottles of moonshine, although he was not sure if he would drink it, he was told to take it anyway as is could be traded for other items.

The day came for Willie to begin his adventure; all of his supplies and his raft were loaded onto the back of a wagon which was pulled by Jacob and Fig. Ma Cahill stayed at home and Jane went with Willie on the wagon so that she could return it and the mules back to the house. Ma Cahill was very upset to see Willie go, but she knew that all he wanted to do was seek adventure. She waved him off with a handkerchief in her hand, and tears in her eyes.

Fanny felt angry because Willie was getting a good send off and hated the way Ma Cahill fussed over him. She also hated the fact that he was off on an adventure and was a free spirit. She appeared to be full of evil but hid it well, although Ma Cahill could see it in her and was noticing it more each day.

For some reason, Fanny decided that she was going to cause as much disruption to Willie's adventure as she possibly could. Maybe her job at The El Tovar Hotel was not a bad thing after all she would be able to gain easier access to the Canyon from there to "help" Willie along his way.

Willie's journey was to start from Lees Ferry just below the Glen Canyon Dam at Lake Powell, Page Arizona. It took four days for them to get to Page. When they arrived they set up a small camp for the night so that they could rest. They enjoyed a meal cooked on a camp fire, and talked through Willie's plans.

The next day they were up early; Jane helped Willie to launch his raft into the water. It was a beautiful August morning and as he loaded his supplies onto the raft Jane cooked them both breakfast.

Willie had studied different types of raft over the last few weeks and had decided a flat raft with a raised wooden platform would be the best idea, he also made storage compartments down the length of each side of the raft to store his supplies and help to keep them dry. He covered everything with tarpaulin, which would also double up as shelter for him when he needed it. He had made a set of oars and strapped one to each storage compartment to keep them from falling off the raft when not in use.

Willie was very well prepared, and had packed supplies based on the knowledge he had gathered from reading about previous tales of Canyon exploration. He had no form of communication to rely on and he knew that once he started his journey through the Grand Canyon the walls would consume him in every way possible, he was not afraid just wary of the possibilities and dangers which would confront him.

Jane and Willie sat on the back of the wagon and ate their breakfast, the coffee and cowboy biscuits went down a treat and so did the thick rashers of bacon. Wille breathed in the fresh air which tasted of the Canyon and had slight bits of sandstone in it which had been brought on the fresh morning breeze. He was very excited and couldn't wait any longer to start his journey.

He gave Jane a hug and thanked her for her help. She told him he should set off and she would clear up the breakfast things and pack them on the wagon. He climbed aboard his well supplied raft and un tied it, he used the oars to gently push the raft away from the river bank, it gently floated on its way down the Colorado River. He waved to Jane who was standing on the bank and kept waving to her until she was out of sight.

The sun was shining on the river and Willie felt so free, he loved the feeling of floating and being carried into unknown territory, he knew the water was quite high and that he could relax a little before he encountered his first rapid. As he sailed his raft along, the walls of the Canyon became steeper, there was a feeling of slight in trepidation as he realised the power and hugeness of his surroundings. At the same time he was in awe of the beauty, he could never have imagined how beautiful this could have been. The colours of the Canyon walls were constantly changing as though dancing with the sound of the river, purple, red, pink, orange and different shades of each of those colours were teasing his eyes as he watched. The walls seemed animated with colour and each second they changed, small rainbows danced across the water as though they were in competition with the Canyon walls for providing entertainment through colour. Willie wondered if this display was a welcome or was it the Canyon luring him in, mesmerised, he floated on and tried to write down everything he saw, heard and felt.

Every so often there was a lovely sandy beach which was slowly lapped upon by the gentleness of the river. It was so beautiful and Willie felt as though he belonged in the Canyon. As he looked up at the consuming walls he saw Big Horn sheep native to the Canyon watching him with interest and curiosity. He lay back on the raft with his hands supporting his head and relaxed, he slowly sailed on he was enthralled by the constant array of surprises the Canyon revealed to him, the opening of each contributory canyon and the mystery which they must have hidden in their depths.

Willie soon passed under the Navajo Bridges at Marble Canyon [Marble Canyon being the sixty mile introduction to the Grand Canyon] and looked up to see the huge structures crossing one side of the Canyon to the other, he drifted slowly underneath. Willie was under a spell. He was taken in by everything he had seen and at this very moment he could not think of anywhere else he would rather be.

By midday it was very hot and Willie had been travelling down the Colorado for four hours, he knew that he would be coming to his first rapid very soon so he decided to pull into a sandy beach and have some lunch and coffee before becoming acquainted with Badger rapid. He tied the rope of the raft to a rock and took out what he needed for lunch, sat on the sandy beach and ate and drank while totally enjoying the complete solitude which was the Canyon.

Willie packed away his belongings and stepped aboard his raft, he was very excited, and although slightly daunted at the thought of his first rapid, knew that he had to tackle whatever it threw at him. As he floated in silence he was well aware that he would soon be challenged.

Suddenly the silence was interrupted by the unmistakeable roar of water, Badger Canyon was coming up and its contributory waters were creating the Badger rapid, there was no turning back and Willie was as ready as he would ever be, he could see the water bubbling up and showing its unwelcoming hospitality in the form of white froth and foam. He had only read about what he had to do and now here he was alone and battling a monster.

As he approached the rapid, he could see the tops of some of the rocks, there was a clear path which he could follow but he also knew that some rocks may be hidden as the rate of water flow was high. Taking one of his oars, he decided to feel his way through to see where the rocks were. Suddenly he was thrust forward as the strength of the rapid took hold. Willie knew he must not let the rapid get the better of him. He must calm down and use every bit of knowledge he had, he was confident enough to let the river take him where it wanted him to go and try to ease his raft through when he could.

He rocked fiercely back and forth but kept in control, his raft was doing well and the oar managed to stay strong against the rocks, it was thrilling but at the same time terrifying, the rapid was huge and seemed to consume him and his raft without mercy. The waves were way above his head and he could not help but feel very small and insignificant. As he battled on through the rapid he could see the calm water ahead and felt a sense of relief, he bravely rode the rest of the rapid through instinct and eventually reached the other side.

As the water calmed Willie gave a sigh of relief, he looked around and noticed that everything was as it should be nothing had been damaged or lost. But he also realised something else, based on the accounts he had read the rapids were to get worse as his journey continued. This one was a baby.

CHAPTER THREE

Willie sailed along; he was very happy, but also rather apprehensive about the next rapid. He knew he could do it as long as he focused his mind, and remembered everything he had read about other people's experiences. The next rapid was soap creek rapid, Willie decided that once he had made it through he would get as close to the next one as he could, but set up camp and get a good night sleep before attempting it.

Soap Creek rapid is said to be unrunnable. Emery and Ellsworth Kolb, who are very famous Grand Canyon names because of their river running photography, had scouted Soap Rapid one evening in 1911, they both took a turn to conquer the rapid only to each be thrown into the Colorado and have to swim to shore in the failing day light.

Willie knew this was going to be a challenge and there was nothing he liked more than that. He was a gutsy little guy, but he also knew he had to be sensible because he was alone; therefore he would scout the rapid first too. He also knew that if he fell into the water he would have a better chance of survival if he was wearing very little clothing because the water of the Colorado is so thick with the silt from the rock which it grinds down; that his clothing would become so heavy it would drag him to his death. He wore a string vest the holes would be too large for the silt to cling to and he wore a pair of very tight underpants which left very little to the imagination and that was when they were dry.

Willie had prepared himself for Soap Creek Rapid the best he could and soon he could hear the roar of water which was becoming familiar to his ears, Soap Creek Rapid was on the way. Willie was very nervous and thought it would be a good idea to moor the raft and have a good look at the Rapid while he could still get ashore.

He floated in and stepped onto the sand, he tied the rope to a rock and walked as far as he could towards the rapid to see what he was going to face.

The rapid was very noisy and fierce; it seemed to go on forever stretching further than he could see. It didn't look any worse than Badger rapid though and he was confident that he could make it; after all he hadn't scouted Badger he had gone in without giving it a thought. This time he knew what he was facing.

He made his way back to the raft and set off from the shore. He began to tense a little as the water began to bubble up and get whiter, then he felt it, the force of the water took the raft and bounced it up and down fiercely. Willie held on tightly to the ropes which he had attached around the sides and rode the white angry waves with as much energy as he could muster. He was thrown from side to side and up and down he was splashed and soaked.

Suddenly he felt the raft dip as though he was on a roller coaster the bottom of the raft was down so low he was practically vertical and the waves of the rapid were all around him like walls. Willie was terrified and freezing cold because of the surrounding water, he felt a warm sensation on his legs; he had no idea where it was coming from but was grateful for it all the same.

Finally after holding on for his life, the rapid seemed to become less aggressive and allowed Willie to pass through it. With a little help from the oars he was able to push the raft away from the protruding rocks.

Willie was spat out of Soap Creek Rapid, he was exhausted and floated to the side of the river bank; he was not out of trouble completely though as he became trapped in an eddy which spun him around and around on his raft to the point that he vomited everywhere. Once he had gained his composure, he realised that the only way out of this was to try and get off the raft, head towards shore and pull the raft with all his might. The shore was not far and

21

if he jumped as far as he could with the rope around his waist he may just be able to reach the sandy bank and make it to dry land.

With all of his might he jumped, his little legs like loaded springs as they launched him off the spinning raft. With great strength he landed just before the shore and only needed to swim a short distance to the sand. He immediately took control of the rope so that he didn't get pulled back into the river; he pulled with all his strength to get the raft out of the eddy. He pulled and pulled but he was really struggling. He was just about to give up and collapse when the raft moved and he was able to pull it ashore. Willie looked around to look at the raft, and was faced with a most unusual sight.

Stood behind him was a mule who appeared to be smiling, Willie knew he had not had any alcohol and wasn't showing any signs of being dehydrated, so was sure he was not imagining what he saw. The mule had the rope in his mouth and had helped to pull the raft out of the eddy. Without thinking Willie thanked the mule, the mule responded by telling Willie that he was very welcome and that he would be happy to accept a drink of moonshine and a biscuit as a way of payment as he had not eaten for two days.

Willie decided that he would set up camp where he was, and asked the mule to join him, the mule told him that his name was Albert but people called him Butt for short, he liked all sorts of food, coffee and moonshine. Willie took what they needed from the raft while Butt gathered some wood for a fire.

In no time at all they had made a very comfortable camp for the evening and both sat next to the fire. Willie made some coffee and biscuits and handed some moonshine to Butt. He stared at Butt wondering if it was a dream. He was sat in front of a mule that was eating biscuits and drinking coffee while cracking open a bottle of bootleg moonshine with his teeth, then Butt poured some moonshine into his coffee. But hell he was a walking talking Ginger biscuit so who was he to question.

Butt sensed that Willie was wondering how he could talk. He explained to Willie that because he was not a complete human, he could understand animals when they spoke. A full human would only hear the usual animal noises. Some full humans who were very special could also understand animal talk. Willie thought that was awesome, that meant that Fanny and Jane could also understand animal talk.

Willie was exhausted but he had warmed up next to the fire. The warm sensation which he had felt on his body during the rapid was caused by him pissing himself with fear so he was smelly too. He decided to heat some water on the fire and have a nice wash, after his wash he put on his spiderman pyjamas and got into his sleeping bag. Butt lay down next to the fire and nodded off, his lips rattled over his teeth while he snored in a deep sleep. The fire was slowly dying out and Willie was beginning to get cold, so he shuffled over to Butt and snuggled up to his belly which was furry and warm.

The night sky was as black as ink and full of stars. The Colorado rambled passed them gently as though it too was exhausted from Soap Creek rapid. The next morning, Willie woke up slowly and opened his eyes, for a moment he forgot where he was. He sat up and was welcomed by the beautiful colours of the Canyon and the warmth of the sun which was touching his little body. It really did feel good to be alive.

Then came the fright, he had forgotten all about Butt who was sitting near the shore looking out at the water, Willie jumped like hell when he saw him, then remembered that he had been very good company.

Butt saw that Willie was awake, stood up and walked towards him, he gave Willie an affectionate smile revealing his huge yellow teeth. Willie swore that Butt actually laughed, his nose moved up and down and his lips rattled over his teeth as he made a hissing squeaking noise.

Willie poked the smouldering embers of the fire and put on some wood to give it enough life to heat a pot of coffee. He mixed up some cowboy biscuits and cooked them over the fire Butt was very hungry and thirsty. Willie poured them both a coffee; Butt looked at his coffee and turned his head away. Willie was confused for a moment, but realised that he had forgotten to add a shot of moonshine. He leaned over and tilted the bottle of moonshine towards Butt's mug. At that very second, his tail caught Willie on the elbow of his pouring arm and rather a lot more moonshine went into the coffee than Willie had intended. Butt told Willie that he had a special name for coffee laced with moonshine, he called it "Star Butts" he said it was named after himself, and because you usually woke up looking at the stars, your own butt, or someone else's if you drank too much of the stuff.

Butt the mule

They sat and enjoyed their breakfast; Butt was a little wobbly when he stood up to stretch his legs, Willie packed up the camp and made the fire safe. He put everything onto the raft and was ready to leave. He told Butt that he was welcome to join him if he wanted too but he would have to walk along the shore because is hooves may damage the raft. Willie boarded the raft and set off on his second day down the Colorado River while Butt happily trotted along the shore very pleased that he had a new friend so share the Canyon with.

Butt had lived down the Canyon for years, since he was a young foal. His mother had given birth to him on the rim and had kept him warm through the harsh plateau winter until they were able to return to the Canyon in the spring to enjoy the warmth and protection it offered.

When Butt's mother died the poor little guy wandered about looking for company and the odd bit of food and coffee from hikers and river rafters. He had picked up his nasty habit of drinking moonshine from an old man who had wandered the Canyon for years just for the heck of it. The old man also used to chew tobacco; however Butt could not stand that filthy habit, he preferred beef jerky.

During the winter, Butt like other animals and sensible humans made his way back to the plateau where it was a little easier to find food and shelter. He enjoyed that because he got together with other mules and they would share stories. They all had bottles of moonshine and beef jerky which they had appropriated by various means. In the summer he wandered the bottom of the Canyon alone so he didn't have to share any good fortune he came across with any other mules.

As he trotted along Butt had a huge smile on his face, he did like Willie a lot, there was something very sweet about him and he did smell of ginger which was such a lovely homely smell. It was a little while before the next rapid, so Willie decided to make the most of the calmness of the water and relax. Every now and then Butt would let off one of his laughs which sent his gums flapping over his teeth and Willie would chuckle to himself, he did appear to be a very happy mule.

As the sun shone down and warmed the Canyon it became extremely hot the thermometer on the raft recorded that it was 112 degrees he was baking. He lay on the raft and thought about how lucky he was to have such an adventure, he knew that once this was over he would have to find a new adventure because it was in his DNA to be outside.

The next Rapid was House Rock Rapid, Willie knew from researching he would have to take this one from the right hand side because a large hole forms on the rapid at most water levels on the left. Before he got to the rapid, he and Butt decided it would be a good idea if one end of a length of rope was tied around Willie and the other end to Butt so if he fell off the raft he could be pulled ashore.

After a while the sound of bubbling water could be heard and Willie knew he was approaching the rapid. Butt started running up and down like a lunatic at the anticipation, he had the rope in his mouth and Willie had to tell him to calm down before he pulled him off the raft and into the water before he had even reached the rapid. As he approached he used the oars to position himself to the right hand side and was immediately consumed by the force of the water into the rapid.

The noise of the water was deafening but Willie could still hear Butt yelping with excitement. The raft rolled from side to side, Willie secured the oar to the raft and held on tightly to the ropes attached either side. Riding the rapid like a cowboy rides a bucking bronco, he came out the other side with adrenaline pumping through his little body, he had completed one of the so called most memorable rapids of the Colorado.

Butt was so excited he rolled around on the shore laughing and kicking his legs, he had never seen anything so thrilling and wished so much that he could have been on the raft.

CHAPTER FOUR

Willie knew that coming up next was a set of rapids called the roaring 20's, he was prepared and confident. He was worried that it would be a struggle for Butt to keep up and had to think what to do. The water was still quite high and sometimes along the shore there was not enough space for Butt to move around the rocks although he could climb over them, if he should stumble then he could land in the water and take Willie with him.

He thought that maybe they could try Butt on the raft while the water was calm to see if it would take his weight and if it did they would ride through the rapid together. He could see how excited Butt was about the rapids and did feel bit mean not sharing the experience with him.

Willie made his way to the shore and tied up the raft. He decided it was lunch time and that they should have a rest and re fuel themselves. He lit a small fire and made a pot of coffee, boiled some water and cooked rice and vegetables. Butt had his fill of Star Butts coffee, then lay in the sun for a while dreaming. Willie was feeling tired too so he lay down and had a nap. He felt so relaxed; this truly was a lovely place to be.

Just as they were snoozing peacefully, there was a rumbling noise. Neither of them took much notice because they thought it was the river. Suddenly a huge rock tumbled down the Canyon wall followed by several smaller ones. Butt jumped up, put his teeth around Willie and pulled him away from the path which the rocks were taking.

Willie was a bit disorientated as he had been enjoying a nice sleep and wondered why he was being dragged by Butt. Then he saw the rocks. Butt explained to him that this was one of the worst dangers of the Canyon. Falling rocks gave no warning and they killed and injured many people. Willie was very pleased Butt had been there to save him.

Just above them on a ledge out of their sight, was a small figure, it was wearing a cloak and its head and face were hidden. Just under the cloak could be seen a glimpse of a Harvey Girl uniform, Fanny was there. Had the rocks fallen, or had they been pushed?

Willie was a bit shaken. They decided it was time to move on anyway and put everything back on the raft. Willie told Butt that if he wanted to he could see if the raft would take his weight and try the next set of rapids. Butt was so excited that he bucked around in circles on the sand laughing loudly. Willie explained to him that he would not be able to jump about like that on the raft and to calm down; they would have to see if it would take his weight first.

Willie got onto the raft and told Butt to climb on and sit in the middle to disperse his weight evenly. As he put his hooves on the front of the raft it shot forward and he fell off. He picked himself up and tried again. Willie said it would be better if they pulled the raft onto the shore slightly to keep it still while Butt got on. When they did he tried again, this time he managed to get onto the raft easily. The raft would not move now however and Willie was not strong enough to move it off the shore with Butt sitting on it.

He told Butt to move to the other end of the raft. When he did it lifted and drifted onto the river. Willie jumped on and they floated off. Butt moved to the middle and the raft seemed very stable he was so happy to be on board with Willie that he started to whistle through his teeth. He was afraid to move too much because his hooves slipped on the wood and he ended up doing the splits. Willie couldn't stop laughing as he watched.

As they drifted along, Willie thought it would be a good idea to tie some rope to the front of the raft so Butt could lean forward and slip his two front hooves in when they approached the rapid to keep him balanced and safe. Just as he finished securing the ropes and Butt had inserted his hooves, the sound Willie had become accustomed to could be heard again, the rushing of the water The Roaring 20's were here. Willie held onto the ropes and could clearly see the route he needed to take.

They hit the rapid with a bang and went straight into its grip. They were thrown and tossed around like two ants on a match stick. Willie was worried about Butt thinking he would be terrified, but when he looked at him he could see that he was swaying from side to side and enjoying himself very much. Butt turned his head to Willie and he was grinning from ear to ear, his ears were pinned to the back of his head and his eyes were wide open the whites of his eyes were like two golf balls.

Willie laughed so much at the sight of Butt in front of him that he pissed himself again; he couldn't stop laughing and knew that if he didn't stop, he would risk falling off the raft. Suddenly the raft took a nose dive into the water. Willie was thrown forward and flew down the raft and landed between Butts arse cheeks. Butt gave one almighty screech and wacked Willie with his tail. Willie fell back onto the raft and took a few minutes to decide if the water or Butts back end were the lesser of two evils for him to land in.

After what seemed like a life time they came out of the rapids and back into calm waters, they were exhausted. Willie was very embarrassed about where he had landed earlier and didn't want to speak about it, Butt was embarrassed and also didn't wish to speak about it, so they both quietly set up camp and ate their food as though nothing had happened.

It was evident that Butt did love riding the rapids, and he had managed to stay on the raft and not damage it at all so Willie decided that if Butt wanted to he could ride more of them. As they poured out the coffee they talked about the rapids which they had conquered that day, skirting around the embarrassing incident which had taken place.

Willie bravely decided that he would try a bit of moonshine just to see what it tasted like. He poured a bit neat into his mug and knocked it back. Butt looked on with interest as Willie coughed and coughed and fell backwards onto the sand. His legs flew up in the air and he shivered from head to foot. He sat up and looked rather red cheeked.

Butts reaction was to throw his head back and laugh so loud and for so long that Willie was afraid he would not be able to catch his breath. He got up and ran towards Butt so he could slap him on the back. He tripped over and landed face first for the second time that day between Butts arse cheeks. This time the force of the laughter and the sudden insertion of Willie into his behind triggered a massive fart which propelled Willie out with force and he landed on his sleeping bag next to the bottle of moonshine where he had been sitting just a few moments before.

Willie's reaction to this was to drink more moonshine he felt so embarrassed. He was surprised the next one went down quite smoothly. As Butt knocked them back without a flinch to hide his embarrassment, Willie thought that maybe he would get more used to it the more he drank so decided to drink with Butt one for one.

What Willie didn't realise was that Butt was a lot bigger than him and was hardened to the moonshine he had been drinking it for years. Willie was sitting on the ground and was nice and warm the moonshine was going down a real treat, and they talked about everything they could possible talk about.

Butt told Willie everything he knew about Canyon life, Willie told Butt about the possible places which he would like to visit in the future. Butt looked puzzled, Willie suddenly realised that all Butt knew was the Canyon. He had no idea that there was a world out there with so many places and opportunities.

Willie took out some of his books and showed them to Butt. He explained to him about the different continents the countries of the world, and that the world was round and how we managed to stay on it without falling off. Butt was completely mesmerised by all of the new information he was learning and asked lots of questions some of which tested Willie's knowledge and he too learned more because he had to look up the answers.

As the schooling continued and the moonshine slowly moved down the bottle, they became very sleepy. Butt got up to go to the toilet in the river and Willie decided he had better go too before he got into his sleeping bag. As he stood up the moonshine did its job, Willie's little legs collapsed under him and he lay in a heap on the floor calling for his mother.

Butt came over, helped him to his feet and stood him up while he had a pee, Butt didn't even complain when Willie's pee was splashed all over him due to bad aiming and an ill timed gust of wind. Both friends crawled to the sleeping bag, Willie climbed inside while Butt collapsed next to him. Willie thought it was best not to move at all because his head felt like it was being swung around on a stick and he was convinced that it may actually fall off. They both slept and snored loudly while the empty bottle of moonshine lay on the sand glistening in the moonlight.

first moonshine camp night

CHAPTER FIVE

The two friends slept as though they were unconscious. Not even the warm rays of sun stretching through the Canyon woke them. It must have been midday before there was any sign of life from either of them.

First to wake was Butt he was more used to the moonshine and its effects. He slowly rolled onto his back and stretched out his legs, as he did he gave an almighty yelp, he jumped up to see that he had been the victim of a scorpion sting. Although nocturnal this scorpion had been shading in the darkness of Butts shadow.

Butt was in agony the scorpion had bitten him on his left hind leg. Willie jumped up to see what all the fuss was about. As much as he tried to head towards Butt he was swaying all over the place from the effects of the moonshine. He managed to steady himself and crawled over to him. He saw the scorpion on the ground and threw something at it to make it go away. It scuttled off.

Willie got the first aid kit out of his bag and immediately gave Butt an antihistamine tablet. He went to the river and soaked a cloth in the cold water. By the fuss Butt was making Willie knew exactly where the site of the sting was so applied the wet cloth to his hind leg, this was to thin down the poison and prevent it going to his heart in a concentrated form. Poor Butt was in so much pain he didn't know what to do with himself. He sat on the sand and looked very pitiful.

Willie was in no fit state to river run today and poor Butt couldn't, the sting had made him feel very nauseous and the last thing he needed was to be tossed around on a raft. Willie decided they would have a day off to rest and that they were not to drink that much moonshine again.

Willie decided a good breakfast with lots of coffee was the answer so he lit a fire. They didn't sit too close to it because the sun was very hot. Willie went back and forth to check on the biscuits and the coffee every few minutes. He was at this present time seeing three of everything so thought the best option was to go for the one in the middle.

As soon as the food was cooked and the coffee made they sat down to eat so they could soak up as much of the moonshine as possible. Willie poured some coffee into a flask and put some biscuits aside for later so that they did not have to light another fire and they could put this one out because of the heat. Willie asked Butt why he drank so much moonshine when it made you feel so crap. Butt explained that he had been drinking it for years and that he was used to it, he said they possibly had a bad bottle because he had not felt like this since he found a bottle floating in the river one day.

He explained to Willie that because producing moonshine was illegal it was often made from ingredients which should not really be added, that was why it was very rare for two bottles to taste exactly the same. Most bottles taste different unless they are from the same batch and made by the same person. It is distilled by moonlight hence the name, but is rarely aged in barrels. Sometimes it becomes contaminated during the mashing, fermenting or distilling stage or by being stored in unsuitable containers. It may contain dangerous levels of toxic alcohols such as methanol. It has also been known to contain lead because a radiator coil has been used as a condenser.

Butt then explained that the way to see if moonshine is safe is to put some on a spoon and set it alight. You cannot tell if it contains methanol because methanol burns with an invisible flame. If it burns blue then it is a good moonshine, if it burns yellow it is a contaminated moonshine. There is also a saying

"Lead burns red and makes you dead" so if it glows red don't touch it.

Willie and Butt both looked at the empty bottle on the ground. Willie picked it up and noticed that there was a little bit left in the bottom. He poured it onto a spoon and lit it with a match, they both looked on in anticipation . . . it glowed bright blue, phew they were ok this meant only one thing. They had quite simply got totally rat arsed.

At least they knew they were just pissed and not ill. Butt was in so much pain with his leg that he kept groaning and rolling about. Willie felt sorry for him but there was not much more he could do. He knew that it would be at least twenty four hours before the pain subsided.

Willie thought it would be best for Butt to try and sleep as much as he could. It was hot in the sun so decided they should move all of their belongings towards the Canyon wall where there was a small cave. It was not big enough for everything but there would be enough room for Willie and Butt to take shade from the sun. He urged Butt to get up but the poor thing was in so much pain he didn't want to move. Willie told him he had to move or the sun would make him feel even more nauseous. Butt stood up and inched his way slowly to the cave his hind leg was very painful and swollen.

Willie looked through his first aid kit and took two painkillers for his head if he felt better then he could help Butt a lot more. He also gave Butt some painkillers although he did not know if they would be strong enough to help.

He went to the river and filled a canteen full of cold water; he thought that if he could keep the site of the sting nice and cool it may help with the pain. Every time he applied the wet cloth Butt whimpered and groaned but looked at Willie with gratitude in his eyes. Willie settled down next to Butt and told him more tales about the world outside the Canyon. Although Butt was very sleepy he did smile every now and then. He seemed a lot more comfortable. Willie soon gave into the affects of the moonshine and also fell asleep, as the day turned into dusk they both slept off the alcohol and the sting.

The sun disappeared from the Canyon and was replaced by the moon which shone down on them. The peace and tranquillity of the Canyon seemed to be like a lullaby with the water gently playing its tune upon the shore. The morning came slowly and gently, the rays of sun took a little longer to reach the cave but when they did it was gradual and woke Willie slowly and gently.

When Willie opened his eyes he immediately knew he was feeling much better, he stretched out and went for a walk to the river for a pee. When he returned he decided that he would let Butt sleep a little longer while he packed all of his things onto the raft.

As he was sorting out the raft he noticed two people walking along the river towards their camp. Willie thought it would be nice to welcome them and ask if they would like some coffee and biscuits. They waved and Willie waved back. Willie got two mugs ready. He went to wake Butt so he too could greet their guests.

He shook Butt but he would not wake, he shook him again but he just lay still, he felt very cold and was foaming at the mouth. Willie panicked and ran down to the shore yelling for help. He was sure that Butt was dead.

The people he had been waiting to greet ran towards him. Willie tried to tell them what was wrong but he couldn't get the words out, he just pointed to Butt, the people were a man and a woman. The man ran towards Butt while the lady tried to calm Willie down and find out from him what had happened. Willie explained about the scorpion sting. The man reached inside his bag and took out a syringe and a small bottle, he filled up the syringe and gave Butt a shot of what the lady told Willie was antivenin. They didn't know if it would work because it had been so long since the poison had entered his system but it was worth a try.

Willie was so upset he sobbed. The man told Willie that Butt had only survived the night because he had done exactly as he should have done the day before and had helped him all he could. Now all they could do was wait and see what happened. The man was a Park

Ranger vet and he told Willie that as soon as Butt was able to be moved they would call for a helicopter to come and take him to the animal hospital.

Willie paced the beach up and down while the lady made him a coffee and the man looked after Butt. All he could think of was the funny ways in which Butt made him laugh. His awkwardness, his hilarious laugh, the way he spread himself out when he sat down and the way he had faced the roaring 20's with so much vigour and absolutely no fear at all.

Willie had only known Butt for a few days but it felt like he had known him forever and was so upset. Eventually the man came over and told Willie that Butt's situation had improved and he was well enough to travel to the rim in the helicopter. Willie was so happy he cried again. He knew he would miss Butt but he also knew that the animal hospital in Flagstaff was the best place for him.

The man introduced himself to Willie telling him his name was Ben and that the lady was Jan. Ben said that as soon as they could they would get word to him on how Butt was doing or he could call them as soon as he could get to a telephone. Willie wanted to go with them but they told him that he should stay where he was and carry on with his adventure after all it's what Butt would want him to do.

As Willie watched the helicopter make its way to the rim he was unaware that in the shadows behind him the sinister figure of Fanny had been watching the drama unfold. She bent down to the ground and gently picked up the scorpion which had stung Butt, kissed it gently and placed it in her white starched apron pocket. Watching Willie as he tearfully waved goodbye to Butt, she sniggered to herself and walked off in the direction of a Canyon trail.

CHAPTER SIX

Willie knew he had to continue with his adventure but he felt so miserable without Butt. He also felt a something which he had never felt before, he felt lonely. He packed his things onto the raft and secured them, he was not in the right mood for another rapid but knew there were so many more to tackle. Willie gritted his teeth and decide to get on with it after all he was here now and the only way out was through the rapids.

Over the next few days Willie tackled the rapids with much determination, he felt that he was on a mission and was also doing it for Butt. The nights around the campfire were lonely without Butt so he tried to go to sleep early and get up early so he didn't have to sit alone for too long.

After six days Willie was running short of supplies, he knew that meant he was approaching the point where he would have to hike up from the Canyon to Grand Canyon Village to buy what he needed for the rest of his trip. He would be glad of that and thought he may treat himself to a room for the night then hike back down early the next morning.

As the raft floated along gently, he made a list of the things he needed. He was hoping that Jane would be there when he arrived it would be so good to see a familiar face. He wondered if Fanny had started her job at The El Tovar Hotel, he could do with some of her lovely food. He then started to think about Ma Cahill, he missed her a lot.

He realised that he was just feeling a little homesick and not having Butt around was making it worse. Before he reached the part of the Canyon below Grand Canyon Village, Willie knew that he had to face Hance rapid. This rapid was particularly tricky because multiple large rocks constricted the channel and formed powerful hydraulics. Willie realised that he would need to use the oars to get his way passed the rocks he would have to be strong and enter the rapid with a plan, this plan would have to be created quickly as the rapid came into view.

Again came the roar, Willie braced himself and managed to negotiate his way through the rocks his raft did take a bit of punishment but it was mainly superficial. Not long after getting through Hance, he was faced with Sockdolager Rapid named by Major Powell because of the punch it delivers. He went into the rapid without a plan because it was difficult to read, he was tossed about and thrown, immediately a wave came and completely soaked him and the raft was swallowed up by water Willie held on to the ropes with all his might as he was spun around as though he were in a washing machine.

He couldn't control the raft so just let it go. He realised that letting it go was the best option because he could not have fought that fight and won. He was a bit battered and some of his varnish had been chipped but he was alright.

He was out of the rapid he checked the raft and his belongings everything seemed to be intact and nothing was lost. Exhausted, he lay back on the raft and floated where the water took him. He looked up at the sky, the light was fading he really needed to get to shore and set up camp for the night. His clothes were soaking wet, he was hungry and thirsty and he was in desperate need of sleep. He would get up early the next morning and hike to Grand Canyon Village.

He set up camp, changed his clothes and lit a fire. He put his wet clothes near the fire to dry and put on some coffee. He had saved some biscuits from the night before so ate those. It would be lonely without Butt, but Willie thought about the rim and that Jane and Fanny could be just a mile above him, so with that comforting thought he settled down to sleep.

The next morning Willie woke up just as the sun was rising, he packed up his camp and secured everything to his raft. He took two large canteens full of water for his hike, a few biscuits and a bag of beef jerky. He tied the raft to a rock.

The Canyon was only a mile deep but the trails were not strait up so it would take a good few hours to reach the Rim. He was near the Grand View trail so took that one. It was nice to have a walk and stretch his legs. He past hikers on the way up as they made their way down to the unique world which lay in the Canyon.

The sun was getting very hot and Willie was baking, he was a bit worried about the chipped varnish on his legs so when he sat down for a rest and a drink, he took out a small jar he had filled with varnish and dabbed a bit on the chipped areas. It dried very well in the sun and he looked as good as new. He continued his assent and was amazed by the beauty and the views from the trail, every minute the Canyon walls changed colour and it seemed the beauty of this place never failed to amaze. After four hours Willie reached the top of the trail.

He made his way to The El Tovar Hotel and was very pleased to see it. He walked in and asked the receptionist named Patty, if they had a room available. She told him they had just received a cancelation by telephone for a room with a queen size bed and an en suite bathroom. Perfect. Wille walked up the stairs to his room, it really was lovely, the bed looked so comfortable and he had nice fresh towels and shower gel.

He was so hungry he decided to put down his bag and go straight to the restaurant for dinner. When he arrived a lovely young lady named Jessie guided him to a table just by the window which had a fantastic view of the Canyon. Willie ordered himself a cold beer and looked at the menu. He was spoilt for choice and eventually decided to have the Filet Mignon which was served with bacon, mash potato and warmed buttermilk.

While he waited for his food he decided to telephone the animal hospital in Flagstaff to see how Butt was doing. He went to the reception and Patty kindly put him through to the hospital. He spoke to a nurse who assured him that Butt was feeling much better and was eating and drinking. She also told him that he had the most infectious laugh she had ever heard and that everyone who met him loved him.

Willie felt so much better now that he knew Butt was alright, he went back to his table and the waitress brought him his meal. The food was so good he savoured every mouthful. For desert he ordered Divine Fudge Lava Cake which was served warm and swimming in fresh cream. It was so good he thought he had died and gone to heaven. He ordered a coffee and a brandy then sat and relaxed. With his coffee came a lovely buttery biscuit which melted in his mouth, he knew the biscuit had been baked by Fanny, no one made biscuits like she did.

He asked Jessie to get Fanny from the kitchen because he wanted to surprise her. He sat and waited excitedly for her. When she came over to him she smiled and seemed pleased to see him but there was an evil glint in her eye. She went back to the kitchen and brought out another biscuit for Willie. Also from under her starched apron she brought out a small shot glass, she whispered to him that it contained bootleg moonshine.

Willie really didn't want to face another glass of moonshine so he put it to one side when she wasn't looking so he didn't hurt her feelings. Fanny told him about her job at the lodge and that she was expecting Jane to arrive any time. She said that Ma Cahill was well but was worried about Willie and his adventures. He had been away from home for eleven days but it felt much longer. Fanny had been working at The El Tovar Hotel for a week. Jane was making her way to Grand Canyon Village after leaving Willie at Lees Ferry and spending a week at home with Ma Cahill, she had also started her job at the reservation with the Navajo horses. Willie was very excited about them all meeting up again.

Fanny went back into the kitchen to continue working. Willie went outside to watch the sunset. He took the small glass of moonshine with him. As he sat looking down over the Canyon, someone came up to him and asked him if he had some matches, they were camping and needed to light their bbq. Willie reached in to his pocket and took out his matches. He struck one to make sure they were not wet from the rapids, as he did so, he accidently knocked the glass of moonshine over which Fanny had given him and the match dropped to the floor. The moonshine was set alight and turned bright red.

"Lead burns red and makes you dead" Fanny had given him moonshine laced with lead.

At first Willie thought maybe she had no idea what it contained, but then he remembered that Fanny always got her moonshine from home and Ma Cahill always made her moonshine very carefully. The moonshine Willie and Butt had drunk was fine and that came from home. Why would Fanny give him moonshine which could kill him?

Willie was rather disturbed by this and realised he would have to keep a careful eye on Fanny she could not be trusted. The biscuit he ate should be ok because she was serving those to everyone and when it was served to him, she didn't know who it was for.

Willie could not understand how they could all be cut from the same dough and yet Fanny could be so nasty.

He was shocked at what Fanny had done, still in his logical mind, he still realised that she may have innocently come in contact with the poisonous moonshine. Before he had any evidence against her he had to give her the benefit of the doubt, but watch her very carefully.

As Willie sat watching the sun set over the Canyon, he could hear a familiar voice in the distance it was Jane, he was so pleased to see her he jumped up ran to her and hugged her. She was very excited the Navajo had given her a beautiful white horse which she adored the horse was named Floating Cloud. She told Willie all about her job at the reservation and how kind the Navajo were to her. They had so much knowledge and had taught her so much about horses in the short time which she had been there. The women had shown her how to cook the native food, and she showed them the unique way in which she could crack a nut.

She wanted to know all about Willie's trip and how he had conquered the rapids so far. Willie told her about his new friend Butt and how much he had missed him when he had to leave the Canyon.

Willie asked Jane if she had seen Fanny yet, she said she had and that she seemed to be settling well in her new job. Jane also told Willie that something rather peculiar had happened just before Fanny had left home the week before. Apparently a young man had called to the Cahill house to ask Ma Cahill if she would like to buy some fire wood ready for the winter. Ma Cahill saw that the young man had done a fine job on his wood, so decided she would buy it to save her having to chop her own.

He was a very polite young man and very handsome he introduced himself as Tom. Ma Cahill invited him into the house for refreshment. She served him some homemade lemonade and some of Fanny's biscuits. He thought the biscuits were absolutely delicious, and asked Ma Cahill if she had made them. Ma Cahill explained that Fanny had made them and called her in from the kitchen to meet the Tom.

When Tom saw Fanny, he shivered from head to foot and seemed to go rather pale. Fanny responded by walking up to him, grinning and holding her hand out for him to kiss it. She fancied him as soon as she saw him and wanted him. Unfortunately for Tom this was not good news. Out of politeness Tom took Fanny's hand although it was obvious that he was not at all comfortable about it. As his lips touched her skin he pulled back quickly as though they had been burnt. He backed away from her. Strangely, he was drawn towards the kitchen and the smell of her cooking; it was as though it had put a spell on him.

A gentle breeze passed through the house and brought him to his senses he thanked Ma Cahill for her hospitality and promptly left.

Fanny seemed furious; it was as though he had shunned her in some way, like a woman scorned even though they had only just met.

Ma Cahill was very concerned about Fanny's behaviour and told Jane that she feared Fanny was capable of great evil.

"Some people are just born bad" she said.

When Fanny left to work at El Tovar a few days later, her room was spotlessly clean as though she had never lived there and she left during the night without saying goodbye. In the kitchen she left three gingerbread people they all had carefully painted faces but had pins in their eyes two of them were leaning against the wall but the third one was lying on the floor with its legs broken.

Ma Cahill had been deeply upset by her behaviour. A few days later Tom was reported missing from his home in the nearby town of Williams. He had not been seen since he had been at the Cahill house and that was also the night which Fanny had left.

Willie was very worried he didn't know if he should tell Jane what had happened with the moonshine, he didn't want to worry her but Fanny was obviously unhinged.

Ginger Bread Fanny

Jane intended staying at the Canyon for a couple of days and was going to go down to the Colorado to spend some time on the rapids with Willie. She would take Floating Cloud with her to help carry supplies and leave her at Phantom Ranch. Willie told Jane she could share his room but she had already made arrangements to camp because of Floating Cloud she didn't really want to stay at The El Tovar Hotel for the night because she wanted to avoid Fanny. She did say she would be grateful for the use of Willie's shower in the morning however.

They said goodnight to each other and she went off to her tent. Willie was very tired so went back to the hotel. When he arrived Fanny was sat in the lobby, she looked surprised to see him and looked rather cross that he was there, this made Willie suspicious that she did know about the "Red Moonshine"

He decided to act as normal as possible and said goodnight to Fanny, she asked him if he enjoyed his moonshine and he told her that he had accidently tipped the glass over and lost the contents. Fanny got up from her chair and went into the kitchen, seconds later she returned with another shot glass full of moonshine and handed it to Willie, he thanked her and said he would drink it in his room, she said goodnight and he swore he saw an evil glint in her eyes.

When Willie got to his room, he decided to light the moonshine to see what happened, he took a spoonful of it and set it alight, it glowed an unmistakeable red. The result sent a shiver up Willie's spine he could not believe Fanny could do this. He got ready for bed and was so worried that before he went to sleep, he pushed a chair up against the door.

The bed was very comfortable and he slept very well he woke early the next morning because Jane was knocking on the door; she was desperate for a pee and did not want to use the camp toilets because there were loads of spiders in them. Willie let her in and she ran to the bathroom. When she came out she asked Willie to order room service for breakfast because she did not want to eat downstairs with Fanny.

Willie ordered the breakfast and a newspaper so he could catch up with what had been happening while he had been down the Canyon. Jane had a shower and was dried and dressed in time for breakfast. Willie poured the coffee and as he did Jane gasped loudly. Willie asked her what was wrong and she showed him the newspaper. At the bottom of the front page there was a picture of a handsome young man and the heading read

"Young Williams Man Found Alive" Jane was so glad, Tom had been found and had been taken to hospital in Flagstaff, as she read on however she became quiet and her face went white, Willie took the paper from her and read the rest of the story.

Tom had been found by a park ranger after being missing for five days. He was at the bottom of Lava Canyon which was a contributory Canyon leading to The Grand Canyon. Both of his legs were broken and he had a thorn stuck in each of his eyes. Willie felt sick and Jane had already been sick in the bathroom. Willie decided he would have to tell Jane about the moonshine because he was sure that Fanny had had something to do with Tom's misadventure and he knew that they would both have to be very vigilant. When he told her she cried because she was very angry, how could Fanny do such evil deeds such as this?

Willie showered and dressed; as he was packing up his bag a horrible realisation hit him. Fanny had made three gingerbread people, who did the remaining ones represent?

CHAPTER SEVEN

Willie and Jane packed up their belongings and collected the supplies which they needed. They placed them on Floating Cloud and started their decent into the Canyon. They talked about their concerns regarding Fanny and the remaining Gingerbread people. Fanny didn't know many people so who could she possibly have a grudge against. Tom had done nothing wrong he was a stranger passing by who just happened to call on them.

Jane decided that the best place for her and Willie at the moment was in the Canyon. They knew where Fanny was so at least they could keep track of her and she did enjoy her job in the kitchen so was unlikely to move on from there.

They had no idea she had been lurking in the shadows when Butt was being taken to hospital and when the rocks had fallen.

When they got to the bottom of the Canyon Jane gave Willie his supplies and they separated so that he could get back to his raft and she could take Floating Cloud to Phantom Ranch. She and Willie would catch up in a day or two when he reached Phantom Ranch at the bottom of the Canyon which was a gathering place for many people and a popular place to camp. Willie knew that Jane would be safe at Phantom Ranch because there would be lots of people there.

Willie eventually reached the raft. He had mixed feelings about returning, he was ready to continue with his adventure, but Fanny had left him so disturbed that he could not help but worry about what she would do next and what she was capable of. He climbed aboard the raft and pushed away from the shore, it did feel good being back on the Colorado and the adrenaline slowly started to pump through his veins again.

After a good rest the previous night he was ready for the next rapid. The incident with Fanny had made him cross so he faced it with attitude. Grapevine Rapid came and Willie thrashed it, he came out the other side with a new confidence and a new way of mentally approaching them.

After setting up camp that night, he sat before the fire and wondered if there was another place on earth which could rival the Canyons beauty and diversity, if there was he would hunt it down and hope to share the intimacy which he felt he shared here in the Canyon. He had hot chocolate tonight for a change and made pancakes. He was so glad that Butt was well and really missed him around the camp fire he missed the way he made him laugh so much that he pissed himself, even if it did make his sleeping bag smell.

The warmth of the fire and his full stomach soon soothed Willie into a deep sleep, he was very content. However this did not last long, he had a terrible nightmare about Fanny, and she was chasing him with a bottle of moonshine and was repeating the words

"Lead burns red and makes you dead"

"Lead burns red and makes you dead" in the nightmare she burst into flames which turned red but she did not burn just stood in the centre of the flames laughing and chanting "Lead burns red and makes you dead"

Willie woke up hardly able to breath, he was sweating and his heart was pounding so fast he thought it would break out of his chest and run into the river. Although he knew it was just a nightmare it took him over an hour to calm down enough so that he could go back to sleep.

The next morning the nightmare was still vivid in his memory, he was glad he had the river to run and focused on that to keep the memory of Fanny away. It was quite a smooth run to Phantom Ranch and Willie very much enjoyed the day, he caught up with his personal notes and ate while he was floating down the river to save time.

As Willie was relaxing and eating, he noticed something floating in the river in front of him. It was a log but it had a furry bump on top of it, as he approached it Wille could hear a little voice chattering away to itself but it was using the most foul language he had ever heard even Ma Cahill when she was totally wasted had never used language that choice.

Willie discovered that the foul mouth belonged to a beaver; he wondered how anything which looked so cute could know such a selection of words. Willie guided the raft closer to the beaver and asked if it needed any help. The beaver reacted by telling Willie that he was absolutely fine and always floated along the Colorado on the back of a log. Realising the creature was being sarcastic Willie threw him a rope and told him to tie it around the log so that he could pull him closer and get him onto the raft.

The beaver did as directed and within a few minutes he was on the raft cursing the day he was born and everyone he had ever known. Willie poured some fresh water into a bowl and pushed it in front of the beaver, it took the bowl and downed the water in seconds then he asked Willie if he had any moonshine. Willie told the beaver that he did have some moonshine, but he would not be giving him any until he had lined his stomach with some food. The beaver tutted irritated by Willie's comment and told him to pass the damn scram now so he could hurry up and get pissed.

Willie told the beaver that he wouldn't put up with such foul words on his raft and in his company and if he used words like the ones he had heard him use again he would push him into the water.

The beaver mimicked Willie's words and laughed at him. Willie told him he could leave now if he wanted to. Surprisingly, the beaver apologised to Willie and thanked him for his help. He looked rather ashamed, as though the realisation of his ungrateful manner had just dawned on him.

He told Willie that his name was Ichee, and that he had been gnawing at the log to release it from a bigger trunk, when it suddenly gave way and floated down the river with him on it. He had been floating for two days and was exhausted, he had gone through three rapids and his stomach was churning so much that he thought he would never be able to keep food down again.

Willie passed him some biscuits and poured him some coffee from the flask; he told him he was sure he would be able to keep it down. Ichee ate the food so fast he looked like a piranha in a food eating race. He drank his coffee and gave a huge sigh of relief. Willie told Ichee that he would be stopping off at Phantom Ranch and he could drop him off there too if he wished.

Ichee thanked Willie for his kindness and asked if he would mind if he had a sleep, Willie told him to sleep in the middle of the raft in case he rolled into the water while he slept. He made shelter for Ichee with the tarpaulin to keep him out of the sun.

Willie felt very lazy and tired, the sun was so hot and he was very relaxed, he drifted off to sleep as they floated peacefully along. He was woken gently by the raft knocking against a rock; he pushed away with the oar and set off again. Not long after they reached Phantom Ranch.

Jane was very excited to see him again even though it had only been a day since she last saw him. Ichee was still asleep so Willie decided to leave him rest after all he'd had a traumatic couple of days. Jane noticed the shelter on the raft and asked Willie who was under it.

He told her it was Ichee Beaver and that he had rescued him from the river earlier that day. Willie warned Jane that Ichee had a foul mouth but had promised to tone it down although he had a feeling they may need to remind him when he woke because it was a nasty habit which Ichee may not be able to shake off so easily.

Jane laughed and reminded him of Ma Cahill but Willie reassured her that Ichee could out do Ma Cahill any day and that she would have to hear it with her own pair of ears to believe it. Jane and Willie sat and talked for hours. When they were hungry Willie gently woke Ichee so they could all go to the Ranch for food.

When he woke up Ichee immediately belted out a chorus and verse of the vilest obscenities imaginable, it seemed that while he was asleep he did forget his promise to Willie. Jane who was usually open minded was disgusted, she wanted to grab him by the scruff of the neck force soap into his mouth and wash the filth out of it.

Willie could not help laughing at Jane's reaction but she told him not to laugh because Ichee would think he was entertaining them and would not want to part with his filthy habit. Considering himself told off Willie tried to stifle his laughter.

As they walked to the ranch Floating Cloud came walking towards them, she really was an image of beauty she looked so pure and was blessed with a gentle nature. As they got closer Jane warned Ichee that if he used one foul word in front of Floating Cloud she would take out her stitching needle and thread, and stitch his lips together. She looked as though she meant it, Ichee was very ashamed and afraid so put his eyes to the ground and promised to be good.

As they walked to the camp together, Floating Cloud showed a great liking to Ichee for some reason, she kept pushing her nose against him and nudging him gently, Ichee became a bit bashful and quiet. When they got to the Ranch Jane told Willie she had a log cabin ready for them, she said that Ichee was welcome to stay as long as he behaved himself.

They were all hungry so left their belongings in the cabin and went to the canteen for supper. Each of them ordered a different choice of food and put it in the middle of the table so they could try a variety of dishes. They had chicken, beef, cowboy biscuits and pancakes with maple syrup. They finished off with a pot of coffee and Willie opened a bottle of moonshine which he hid under the table. There were lots of tourists there from all over the world but also a lot of Grand Canyon residents and staff.

Every time they topped up their coffee mugs they slipped some moonshine into it, they would have been in trouble if they had got caught and thrown out because they could only drink alcohol which had been bought in the canteen and of course the moonshine was bootleg. Willie was also careful not to let Jane see the moonshine because she did not approve of it at all.

They didn't realise however that because Jane was completely sober she had noticed there was something wrong, Willie who had only been introduced to moonshine a couple of days ago by Butt, had started to slowly slide down his seat as the alcohol was getting the better of him. Ichee was fairing slightly better because he was used to necking down bottles of the stuff, but because he had been floating down the Colorado for a couple of days and had lost some of his body weight, the moonshine was at an advantage. Ichee slowly stood up and started to sing, his voice was brilliant and everyone stopped what they were doing to listen to him. He stood on his chair and then on to the table as people cheered and shouted out requests.

After half an hour he took a break so he could take on some refreshment. Jane was so pleased with him she bought him a nice cold root beer. Ichee didn't want root beer he wanted more moonshine so he excused himself from entertaining everyone for a few minutes and sneaked outside, he went back to the cabin and took a bottle from Willie's bag he opened it and drank it down as though he were drinking water.

He felt fine until he went outside and the cool air hit him in the face then his body seemed to go in the opposite direction to where he wanted it too and his legs turned to jelly. He also had a fit of giggles because he could see all sorts of weird things dancing in front of him.

Ichee Beaver

He managed to make his way back to the canteen and decided he would give them some of his best songs. He walked in and climbed up onto a table, he immediately started to sing but the songs which came out of his mouth were not what anyone expected, the words were utterly filthy and the actions he put to the words were just as bad. Willie who was by now slumped in a chair unable to talk had a look of sheer panic on his face. He tried to get up and grab hold of Ichee but his legs gave way and he landed flat on his face.

Jane went up to the table and grabbed Ichee Beaver, she put one hand over his mouth and the other around his neck, he gasped for breath but she didn't let him go until they were outside. When they got through the door she put him down on the floor, he immediately started to curse so she grabbed hold of him and clamped his mouth shut with her hand again. She told him she was going to make him some strong black coffee and he was going to drink every drop, but first she was going to cure him of his evil tongue.

Jane took him into the communal wash room and strapped him to a chair, for a split second Ichee contemplated telling her he liked kinkiness but thought better of it. She went to the sink and pumped soap into her hand. She walked over to Ichee and held his nose so he had no choice but to open his mouth, he gritted his teeth they were like white shiny barriers desperately trying to protect his mouth but she forced the soap in, it found its way in between his teeth and he spluttered and coughed, he wretched and bubbles blew out of the tiny gaps in his pearly whites.

Eventually he gave in opening his mouth and taking the punishment he so well deserved. Jane got a bottle, filled it with water and emptied it into his mouth to create lather. The soap washed his mouth out clean, but had it washed away the filthy words? Only time would tell. Jane untied him and carried him to the cabin; she made him some coffee and gave him some biscuits to take away the taste of the soap.

Ichee started to sober up he realised he had been very bad and he had broken a promise, he decided he would not drink moonshine again because it made him do very naughty things and the new friends he had made may not like him anymore if he kept getting pissed and misbehaving.

Jane gave him a blanket to sleep on and told him that she was going back to the canteen to get Willie and when she got back he had better be still sitting on the blanket. After what she had just done to his mouth he had no intention of disobeying her.

When Jane arrived at the canteen Willie was slumped over the table muttering to himself incoherently. Jane asked a man from the canteen if he would carry him to the cabin. On the way to the cabin, he kept muttering to himself about Butt, Ichee and red makes you dead.

He was put to bed and Jane made him some coffee, he was so unconscious he didn't drink it and she knew he would suffer more for not drinking it. He turned over in his sleep and muttered something about a teddy bear and then he was silent.

The next morning Jane was up early, she decided to let the two moonshiners sleep a little longer to save herself from having to listening to their hangover complaints. She went to the canteen for breakfast and then sat on the porch and read some of her book.

After a while she decided to ride Floating Cloud down to the river to make sure Willie's raft was alright. It was a beautiful morning and the river looked lovely the world at the bottom of the Canyon was so peaceful and pure; she could see clearly why people loved it so much.

After sitting for a while she realised that Willie and Ichee may be stirring out of their drunken slumber so had better head off to fill them with coffee and pain killers. When she arrived back at the cabin she could not believe her eyes, Fanny was standing over Ichee and was chanting some babble. Fanny didn't hear Jane walk in, and started to make her way towards Willie's bed. Jane was going to shout out but thought she would keep quiet and see what Fanny was going to do.

As Willie slept, she took out a handkerchief and a small knife from her apron pocket and gently scrapped some of Willie's varnish coating from the bottom of his foot, then scrapped the knife to remove some crumbs of gingerbread. She placed her samples in the handkerchief folded it up and placed it back in her pocket. Jane hid behind the chair while Fanny sneaked out of the cabin.

Jane felt sick because she now knew what Fanny was up to. She was adding the DNA from victims to her gingerbread dolls, punishing the dolls, and the person the DNA came from was suffering for real. There was no doubt that Fanny truly was evil and had to be stopped. Jane checked on Ichee and noticed some of his fur had been cut off.

CHAPTER EIGHT

Eventually Willie woke from his moonshine sleep. Jane waited for him to have a coffee and something to eat at the canteen and when he returned she told him about Fanny and what she had seen her do to him and Ichee. Willie felt sick he immediately replaced the varnish on his foot. He didn't know what to say to Ichee because he didn't want to worry him. Ichee would want to go off on his own again soon and Willie would be worried about him he would feel terrible if anything happened to him just because he had befriended him.

He looked at Ichee while he slept and felt very protective over him, Ichee looked so sweet and cute when he was asleep and his mouth was shut, there were no obscenities leaking out he was just furry and cuddly. Jane said she needed to go and check on Floating Cloud, she wanted to make sure that she would be comfortable at the Ranch while she was on the raft.

Jane was leaving Floating Cloud in the care of a Hopi Indian who worked at the Ranch and whose stallion had fathered her; she knew her beautiful horse would be in good hands.

When she got to the stables, Floating Cloud was having a lovely time running about with the other horses, the Hopi who was looking after her told Jane to go and enjoy the river without worrying as he would take good care of her horse. He also told her he was very concerned, he had a feeling that there was an evil force at work which was trying to cause harm to her and her travelling companions.

Jane immediately knew he was referring to Fanny, and told him what had happened with the red moonshine and the gingerbread people Fanny had made. She told him Fanny took a snip of Ichee's fir and had extracted some crumbs from Willie. The Hopi looked very worried and told her that they should all be very wary as she could be capable of anything.

Jane thanked the Hopi for looking after Floating Cloud and went to wake Ichee Beaver so they could get onto the raft. She too thought he looked very cute when he was asleep and although she had punished him for swearing obscenely, she felt an overwhelming urge to mother the furry little git.

Jane woke Ichee and she was expecting him to spill out more foul sentences of filth, but he didn't, he sweetly bid her good morning and smiled showing his sharp, white teeth.

Maybe the soap had done the job and cured him of his affliction. They walked to the river where Willie was waiting for them he had loaded up the raft and was sitting down writing in his journal under the shade of a tree.

Willie helped Jane onto the raft and Ichee climbed on too, he was obviously happy to be travelling with them and looked very pleased when Willie said that he could sit at the front of the raft and keep a look out for the Rapids. As they set off, they felt very excited about the next few days so much had happened in the last part of the Canyon and Willie was wondering what the next part would bring.

As the happy trio floated away from Phantom Ranch, and ill wind blew in their direction and a rustling could be heard in the dry bushes, an evil face appeared the eyes were black and dead, they had no suggestion of emotion at all and a rattling sound penetrated the air. The eyes belonged to something who wanted to cause as much destruction to this river run as possible and it was not Fanny.

Jane played the banjo and they sang as they floated along. They passed lots of people on the way who waved to them and shouted good luck. The Canyon was so big, yet there didn't seem to be a shortage of company everyone seemed to be content and happy in their surroundings. Every so often an organised river trip would pass them, the boats would be full of tourists and people out for as many thrills as they could get. The guides on the tours were all very experienced and had spent many years down the Canyon and running the Colorado.

At night time these groups would sit around a camp fire, eat, drink and share life stories with each other. Each person had a reason for being there, a lifelong ambition, the thrill of adventure and adrenaline buzz which the Canyon had to offer, or sometimes people just needed to get away from life for a while as it had been a bit tough on them.

The guides always had good stories to tell and around a roaring campfire was the perfect place. Each guide had different experiences to share but the main stories of the Canyon were always the same because they were so gripping and true, from fatal accidents to murder the Canyon held more secrets than anyone could ever imagine.

While the first part of the journey for Willie had been quiet, the second part was proving to be rather different. The Canyon became full of life. Helicopters, boats, tourists, and screams of terror as people hit the Rapids were becoming a familiar sound. The helicopters swooped down into the Canyon to give people who did not want to venture in by mule or foot the thrill of an aerial view.

Those who did travel by their own means saw much more. The safest way to travel into the Canyon is by mule because these creatures are very agile and stable; they know the Canyon trails well and can carry what you need. Many people who venture into the Canyon without advice, basic knowledge or common sense, usually end up in trouble.

Water is the main essential they run out of, they totally underestimate the amount of fresh water they need and then expect to find some when they get to the bottom. It has been known that people can wander the depths of the Canyon for days not being able to find a way out, they are usually found dead or half dead.

Willie knew of these dangers because he had read all about the Canyon and had taken advice from people who had lived there all their lives, this enabled him to become part of the environment and enjoy it because he had knowledge and respect. He was aware that the Canyon was very susceptible to flash floods especially at this time of the year.

Most people believe that the Colorado River is responsible for carving the Canyon into the earth, but that is only a part of it. Flash floods carrying devastating amounts of water have broken free boulders and carried them into the Canyon. The boulders and the water crash down consuming everything in their path and constantly changing the shape of the Canyon. This creates new rapids and waterfalls as well as destroying existing ones. Whatever is in the way gets taken by the flood water, including many people, animals and vegetation. Even a small amount of precipitation forty miles up from the Canyon can cause huge flash floods.

Before the next set of rapids Willie told them some of the stories he had read about flash flooding and the victims it had claimed. Jane looked rather alarmed but Willie told her that if they were going to be at one with nature they had to know about the dangers which they faced. Ichee sat and listened fascinated by Willie and his stories.

The next few Rapids were fantastic, they rode through them with all the fun and thrills which were to be expected. Along the banks of the river they could see people who were absolutely soaked trying to dry off as they pulled in after a rapid for a debriefing. Jane had a wonderful time, she loved riding the rapids and Ichee enjoyed it too, he said it was far better being on the raft than having his log tossed.

Willie realised he didn't know anything about Ichee. He asked him if he had a family, Ichee told him that he was just a wanderer, he did come from a very large family but they were completely dysfunctional. Most of them were drunks and criminals. Although he had a foul mouth he knew he had gotten off lightly compared to his siblings.

The problem had been his parents, they were totally irresponsible. They smoked dope and drank copious amounts of beer. They had sixteen children and only one of them was genetically normal.

This was because their parents were very closely related. Ichee was the normal one, because his mother had wandered off one day and become pregnant with him by a stranger, because this stranger was fresh blood Ichee was genetically sound but the trauma of living with mutant beaver brothers and sisters had been so stressful that he had turned to swearing.

Once he told his story, Jane felt very guilty about what she had done to him, but Ichee said that if it stopped him from swearing it would be a great help to him because he couldn't find a decent woman as long as he had a foul mouth.

He went on to explain that he had been in love with a beautiful beaver named Becci, he had been watching her for weeks too shy to make a move, he didn't know what to say to her so he just sat and watched. One day he managed to climb into a tree and he watch her from above. She was a very busy beaver; she rushed around building and creating all day and really did have a fantastic way with the younger beavers.

As he watched her Ichee became a bit wobbly in the tree and fell to the ground. Becci rushed over to help him; Ichee was so put out by his fall that he spat out a string of verbal abuse. When Becci heard this she was so shocked and disgusted that she walked away before Ichee even had a chance to practice some of his nice words on her.

Ichee tried for weeks to get close to Becci but she wouldn't give him the chance. He wanted so much to be given another chance with her but didn't know what to do to get her attention and make amends.

Jane told him that he should not give up; he should keep trying because she knew that he was a very nice Beaver and that there was so much more to him than naughty words. She reminded him that he was a very good singer and had a beautiful voice; maybe the sweetness of that voice could be used to win Becci over.

She asked him if he knew any love songs, he said he did know a lot of Lionel Richie songs because he used to listen to an mp3 player which someone had left near the river once and his greatest hits were on it. Well that was a start. Jane told him to choose a song which he liked the most from the collection and practice it so that when he had the opportunity he could sing it to Becci, once she heard his beautiful voice she would have to give him another chance.

Ichee thought about it and decided it was worth a try. He decided to practice all the songs so that he could choose the right one to suit the situation when it arrived. Willie asked Ichee where he had lived and Ichee told him that he was born in Canada but his family were to be deported due to the trouble they caused. They didn't know where they would be sent so escaped over the border to America so that they could start a fresh life.

Becci was still in Canada and he couldn't go back there in case he was caught so he would have to try and get Becci to come to him somehow. Jane and Willie were determined to reunite the beavers so that Ichee could get another chance. As they floated along between Rapids Ichee sang his little heart out. He sat at the front of the raft and entertained them all the way causing much amusement to others on the river with his furry little head thrown back while he belted out his songs.

When the daylight began to fade they tied up the raft for the day and set up camp. Just a few yards from where they settled were a party of river runners who had passed them earlier and had commented on Ichee's singing. They asked the trio if they would like to join them. Willie thought it would be very nice to have some new company so they made their way to the neighbouring camp.

There were ten people and two river guides, the atmosphere was fantastic, full of excitement and everyone was chattering about the experiences of their trip. Willie took some coffee and biscuits to share, everyone in the camp had contributed something and the food was delicious.

There was also a lot of alcohol and Jane was very worried about Ichee, but he assured her that he would not drink at all he was going to be a good boy, besides he had already had a good look around and there wasn't a drop of moonshine in sight, which was the only thing he had a weakness for. Jane told a lot of stories about the Hopi and Navajo Indians which she had learned from the tribes while spending time with them. Willie told them about Butt and his scorpion bite.

One of the tourists asked them if they had ever come across moonshine, Willie smiled and said that it was surprising the things you came across in the Canyon. Willie was very fascinated by a man named Jon who was visiting from the United Kingdom; he liked his accent and thought that he was a very interesting guy. Jon had been a Police Officer and had recently retired. He was using his pension money to visit a few places in America, travelling alone because he wanted to be able to go where he wanted and when he wanted without worrying about anyone else.

Willie said he would very much like to visit the United Kingdom one day because he had read about it and thought it would be a big change from Arizona. Jon told him he would be very welcome to stay with him anytime he wanted to visit. He told Willie that he was from Cardiff which was the capital of Wales and that the tallest mountain in Wales was Snowdonia. Willie said he would love to climb up a mountain as he was now down inside an inverted one.

The river guides had lots of stories to tell, they told stories which were years and years old and stories which had happened very recently. There were very sad stories, very mysterious stories and some weird stories, but they all shared one thing in common, they were all true to the best of their knowledge.

One of the stories was about a snake which wandered the Canyon floor looking for victims, this snake was evil to the core and would do any job any one hired her to do in return for a supply of fresh eggs. Her name was Vicky or Vicious Vicky as she was commonly known. She had no particular reason to be evil she was just born that way. She sneaked around waiting for an opportunity to do something nasty. She was very difficult to track down and she had several dens so could go from one place to another and know that she had her home comforts, which were a bed made from beaver skin and bird feathers, a supply of fresh eggs and a good view of the Canyon.

Vicious Vicky had a favourite nasty pass time, she loved to lay low on the Canyon trails and bite the feet of the mules as they went past, for this reason a lot of the mules had become terrified of travelling down the Canyon, some of the younger Mules were bitten on their first ever trip down and from that moment had refused to go again.

The main story which gripped every river runner and visitor to the Canyon was that of the missing honeymoon couple Glen and Bessie Hyde. The newlyweds had gone missing when running the Rapids through Grand Canyon in 1928. Their stow was found at rapid 232 in tact with all the supplies on board but they were missing.

There were lots of rumours and speculation but no one ever found out the truth about their disappearance although many believe they were taken by the Colorado, some believe that they may have been murdered, or that Bessie murdered Glen and hiked away to a new life because he changed when he ran the rapids into a man she didn't like. They wanted to hit the headlines as being the first honeymoon couple to complete the 277 miles of the Colorado through Grand Canyon. Sadly they hit the headlines for a completely different reason.

It was a fascinating but sad story, Glen's father never gave up hope of finding them. He spent years and thousands of dollars trying to find an answer, even if it was the recovery of the bodies because he could not stand the thought of never knowing what had happened to his son.

Everyone around the camp fire was silent; the story was very moving and sad. It proved that the Colorado and the Canyon were a force to be reckoned with. They say that the Colorado rarely gives up its dead. It takes a lot of lives.

Ichee was very happy, he had not had a drink only coffee and because of that he was able to join in more and enjoy the company and the stories. He could sit upright, hear and see what was going on. Being sober was not a bad thing after all and the best thing was that the next day he did not have a head like a stone in a washing machine.

CHAPTER NINE

Everyone settled down in the camp and the River Guides showed them how to check for scorpions and dispose of any which they found. They advised that socks were put over shoes and boots to prevent the scorpions entering them at night, most victims were bitten on the foot from their shoes being a scorpion bed. Willie sat up for hours chatting to Jon about his police days, but Ichee, Jane and everyone else slept like logs.

Willie thought he could hear something close by, it sounded like a rattle and in the light cast by the campfire, he could see the dry bush moving very slightly, the air was still so it was not a breeze which caused the movement. Suddenly he heard a hiss and so did Jon, they both jumped up and walked over to the bush very slowly and quietly. As Jon parted the bush they discovered the evil face of a rattle snake, she did not even try and move away just brazenly raised her tail and rattled it at them.

Neither of them moved they knew who it was it was Vicious Vicky, Willie wanted to catch her because he could now see with his very own eyes how evil she really was, her eyes were like black shiny beads which shone in the light of the fire and she seemed to grin with the look of the devil. Jon and Willie went to wake one of the Rangers so they could warn everyone, but when the three of them walked back to Vicky, she was gone.

By the description they both gave, the River Guide was able to confirm that it was Vicky they had seen, and that they would have to be very careful, once she knew she had been seen, she could be even worse.

As they settled down to sleep Willie could hear the rattling again coming from where Jane and Ichee were sleeping. He jumped up and ran to them. Sliding all over them both was Vicious Vicky she was hissing and rattling as though she were possessed. She raised herself up and was just about to clench her teeth into Jane when the River Guide netted her from behind. Vicky struggled and hissed she was hateful and very scary to look at. It was obvious that Jane and Ichee were being targeted deliberately but they had no idea why.

Vicky was put inside a wooden box with air holes in it and it was sealed down. The rangers kept these boxes for the very purpose of containing wild life which was either a danger to people or needed help.

At last Willie was able to settle down to sleep. The next morning one of the River Guides confirmed that he had found one of Vicious Vicky's hide outs and had discovered something very strange inside. The den contained the usual items they would expect and piles of eggs, but the strange thing about it was the eggs were all in boxes labelled

"The El Tovar Hotel"

How on earth did Vicky manage to get those boxes down to the Canyon?

Willie and Jane felt sick; Fanny was unable to follow them through the Canyon to unleash her evil intent, so she had paid Vicious Vicky to do it for her. The River Guides were very puzzled about the egg boxes, but also very happy that they had caught the infamous Rattle Snake, that meant that the mules could enter the Canyon without fear and it was a safer place for many others too.

It was sad to see such a beautiful creature being captured and removed from its environment but she needed to be examined to see why she was behaving in such a way, she could be ill or in need of mental health treatment. The River Guides radioed Grand Canyon Village and a helicopter came and took Vicious Vicky away.

Willie, Jane and Ichee thanked the River Guides for the lovely evening and everyone else for their company. Before they left one of the River Guides told Willie that they were very irresponsible not wearing life jackets and handed him some which were surplus to their needs. Willie thanked him then took Jon's details and promised to be in touch. They boarded the raft again and set off for another day on the River. There was great relief that Vicious Vicky had been detained, but they both had a feeling that Fanny would not let the small set back stop her unexplainable mission to cause harm to them.

Their journey took them passed some of the trails leading from the Rim to the Canyon floor they were near Tonto trail and as they passed the point where Tonto Trail hikers would be making their way to the river, Willie heard a laugh which unmistakeably belonged to Butt.

He looked around searching for him, and then he saw him running towards the river with great excitement. His tail was dancing in the air and his lips were once again forced over his teeth by a huge smile his ears were moving back and forth as though someone was pulling them with an invisible string. Willie pulled the raft into the shore and jumped off. He ran towards Butt and it was as though they were in slow motion as the two friends were re united.

Jane and Ichee had tears in their eyes as they watched the moving scene unfold before them. Jane and Ichee got off the raft and went to greet Butt. They thought he was lovely. Wille took the flask from the raft and they all sat down and had a coffee and introduced themselves. Butt told them all about his time at the hospital where he had been totally spoilt and had enjoyed the food very much. He was feeling better than ever and ready to continue down the river if that was alright with Willie. Willie was so happy to have Butt back and told him he could not wait to ride the Rapids with him again.

They told Butt about Fanny and Vicious Vicky, he was very glad that she had been caught because she was so nasty to the mules. Butt ate some biscuits and made himself a Star Butts. Ichee was very good and didn't even sniff the cork when Butt pulled it out of the moonshine bottle.

They had a good chat, then got back onto the raft and continued their journey. Ichee, Butt and Willie got on board while Jane untied the raft. Willie was so happy to have his friend back again. They floated along the river for a few hours and enjoyed the hive of activity which the Canyon had become. Willie knew that the next big rapid which they would be approaching would be a very difficult one; it was the notorious Crystal rapid. They would get through Crystal and then set up camp for the night because he was sure they would need a rest after this one.

As they enjoyed listening to Ichee singing, Willie asked Jane to make sure that the ropes were tight and that all the supplies were firmly secured in preparation for Crystal rapid. He handed out the donated life jackets, put one on himself, and told Ichee and Jane that from that moment on they were to be worn at all times while they were on the raft. Unfortunately there was not one big enough for Butt, so they tied eight plastic bottles around his body to act as floats in case he fell into the water. Once all checks were done he told them that Crystal could be a vicious Rapid, they had got through Hance rapid with a fight and this one was the same if not worse.

Crystal Rapid was formed in 1966 when a flash flood washed debris into the Colorado from Crystal Canyon. There are several large holes followed by a rock garden at the bottom of the rapid on river left. Willie was not sure how he would approach and run this one. He decided it may be a good idea to scout it first to see what they were up against.

As he prepared to moor the raft so he could get off and scout, they were suddenly pulled to the left with force, Willie tried to fight it and struggled to get in control of the raft but it was no use they were in the grip of the water, he had made a mistake he had underestimated the distance to Crystal Rapid he had not heard the roar because of the singing on the raft and the noise of the helicopters up above but the rapid was here and it was too late to do anything. He shouted to the others to hold position and rope down.

Butt assumed his place at the front; his face was a picture he was so much looking forward to his first Rapid since being removed from the Canyon. As soon as he saw the white water he screeched with excitement, as usual his ears were back, his teeth gritted and his eyes as large and as white as golf balls. Ichee and Jane roped themselves to the sides. Willie didn't have time to un tie an oar so he just grabbed hold of the rope and clung as tight as he could.

They hit the rapid with a massive thump which sent the front of the raft into the air, Butt was almost vertical in front of Willie and his legs desperately scrambled around looking for something solid to give him stability. His hooves were scratching at the log raft as he tried to gain control of his body which was being thrown about like a ragdoll. Finally to the relief of Butt the raft landed back on the water but it was with a slap and he banged his chin on the floor.

Willie was relieved that they hadn't been tossed off, but before he could blink they were heading into a hole, the front of the raft was plunged forward and Butt found himself in the complete opposite position to what he had been in seconds before this time his front hooves battled to keep him from falling over the front of the raft the ropes rubbing hard on his skin. Jane was holding on but being thrown about violently and Willie knew that he had to hang on and pray that they all made it through this rapid.

Willie looked towards Ichee, he looked terrified, although his paws were fixed inside the rope loops, he was so afraid that his teeth were also gripped onto the rope and they were chattering with fear. Like little knives each tooth was slicing through the rope without him realising and suddenly the fibres of the rope pinged free and he was thrown forward.

He tried to grip onto something but he passed everything with such speed that he did not get chance to take hold. Butt was in front of him and as Ichee hurtled towards the front of the raft all he could see was Butts rear end.

Not wanting to be a furry Butt plug, he tried to alter his route by stretching his legs forward trying desperately to use them as breaks, in doing so, his sharp claws scraped along the logs making a hell of a screeching noise. Suddenly he hit a knot in the wood and was propelled forward. He flew into the air over Butts head and with great speed cleared the raft completely landing in the Colorado.

The raft surged forward with great velocity carrying the three remaining pals on board. Poor Ichee was in the water and his chances of survival with his furry coat and the dangers of Crystal rapid did not look good. There were river runners downstream who could see the trouble the raft was in so prepared to help them as soon as possible. As they neared the end of the rapid it did start to give back control of the raft to Willie although a little reluctantly.

Exhausted, they lay on the raft and waited for it to stop tossing around. Willie immediately started to call for Ichee he couldn't see him anywhere and panicked. The water was white and foamy so Ichee's brown fur and life jacket should have been visible if he was in the water, but he could not see him. If he was under the raft he would be in trouble because the raft was flat and there would be no air pocket for him to breathe. Jane called for him over and over in a panic and Butt screeched at the top of his voice. The raft was thrown out of the rapid by the hydraulics caused by the remaining holes and rocks and it floated towards the shore.

Willie jumped off the raft and ran back up towards the rapid. He stood on a rock and looked out into the swell to search for any sign of Ichee. He called and called but his voice was drowned by the noise of the water. He walked back to the raft with his eyes looking down to the floor. He could not look at Jane who was sobbing uncontrollably as she tied up the raft he just sat on the sand. Ichee was gone the Colorado had taken him.

Willie was distraught and Jane sobbed, Butt hadn't known the little guy for long but he cried too. Jane helped to untie Butt who had been caught up in some extra rope and the three of them sat on the shore unable to speak. The river runners who had watched them come out of the rapid approached them, it was a group of six men and three women, the men said they would go and look for Ichee and the women wrapped blankets around Willie, Butt and Jane and made them a coffee with lots of sugar in.

They continued to search the river until it was dark and then came back for torches so they could look some more. There was no sign of Ichee. Willie knew that he was probably so full of silt he had sunk to the bottom and would never be found. Normally if rescuers looked for a body in the Colorado, they set off small explosions under water to try and get the body to float to the top, but Willie thought that Ichee should be left in peace.

That night they joined the other river runners and were fed and looked after by them. One of them was a Park Ranger and he told Willie that he would have to report Ichee as missing in the morning. Willie could not sleep that night he felt so guilty he wished he could turn back time. He really should have scouted Crystal rapid first and now Ichee was dead. He felt angry too, was this Fanny's doing? Had she made a doll of Ichee when she cut his fur and made this happen?

Butt managed to sleep because he drank a bottle of moonshine and Jane cried herself to sleep. The next morning Jane woke early and saw that Willie had finally fallen asleep so decided to leave him where he was for a while, she didn't know if he wanted to continue with the trip or go home.

Jane had an idea; she thought that if they at least continued the trip to Havasu Falls maybe they could do a memorial service at Beaver Falls for Ichee which was on the way. Such a beautiful place would be perfect. When Willie woke up she asked him if he wanted to continue the trip, she told him her idea about the memorial but said that if he didn't wish to continue they could hike out of the Canyon after Havasu falls and head for home.

Willie was very moved by Jane's idea and said that he would decide if they were going to stay or leave the Canyon when they reached Beaver Falls and had the memorial. He asked the Park Ranger if he would put a notice in a newspaper so that anyone who knew Ichee and wanted to attend the memorial could do so.

It would probably be about four days before they reached Beaver Falls so it would give anyone who knew Ichee time to get there. After some breakfast and coffee they boarded the raft and continued on the river. They were all very quiet and very sad. There was no one to sing Lionel Richie for them.

Butt assumed his position at the front of the raft his eyes were so sad and his head was so heavy with grief he could hardly lift it. Willie went through the motions but did not really have the heart to do any more river running. Jane sat and cried.

It was a horrible day and they were glad they didn't have any major rapids to run because they didn't have the strength to run them. Every time another river running group saw them, they stood at the river edge or to attention on their vessels, removed their hats and bowed their heads in respect for Ichee. He had become famous and loved for his floating entertainment.

The next few days and nights were very lonely and sad but they did laugh and smile at the memories they had about Ichee. They had only known him for a short while but the little guy had so much character that they felt they had known him for much longer, he had left his mark in many ways. Jane felt good that she had cured him of his swearing before he had reached the pearly gates and met Saint Peter.

As they drifted along the river, they made plans for the best memorial they could give him.

CHAPTER TEN

The journey to Havasu Creek was a long one but relatively smooth, there were some minor rapids but they took advantage of the high flow and drifted along peacefully. Jane played the banjo and they tried to cheer themselves up. Jane said it would be a nice idea if they could sing one of the songs which Ichee loved to sing at his memorial, they practiced a few songs, it did help to lift their spirits.

The night before they were due to arrive at Havasu Creek, they again set up camp next to a river running group, this group was also going to Havasu Falls. The guides on this river trip were aware of what had happened to Ichee and told Willie that some of his friends and family had been contacted and would do their best to be at the memorial service.

That night Willie was again very glad of the company of others. They ate lovely food and drank freshly brewed coffee. Willie decided that it would be polite to give something in return to the group for their hospitality so went to the raft and took out a bottle of moonshine from the storage compartment.

The river runners who were mostly British could not believe their eyes as Willie pulled out the cork from the dodgy looking bottle and poured each of them out a shot into their tin mug, as he did so he whispered to each of them to pretend it was gin because they would get into trouble with the River Guides if they were caught with bootleg. The runners thought that moonshine was a myth; none of them had actually seen any before they absolutely loved it, not so much the taste but the fact that it was bootleg moonshine.

Every time the River Guides turned their backs the bottle was passed around the group, the contents knocked back in one leaving a sudden gasp for breath and eventually a smile on every mouth it entered.

Of course Butt was not going to be left out, he had his fair share of moonshine and started to laugh and fall over from his very unusual sitting position which caused roars of laughter around the camp. As he joined in with the laughter, his lips pulled up over his teeth as usual and he looked so funny that everyone fell about. One of the older ladies walked off discretely as she had pissed her pants laughing at Butt and had to get changed.

Jane took out her banjo and played and everyone sang along, Willie danced and when the music stopped for Jane to have a drink, Willie told everyone that they should dedicate the fun they were having that night to their dear friend Ichee Beaver.

The River guides came and sat with them, so the moonshine had to go away but they told some more really good Canyon stories, they also told some spooky stories too which had everyone rooted to their spot. Before they went to bed they were told a lighter hearted story about a lovely mule named Blighty who famously lived down the Canyon and on the rim for years he was famous for being a very good friend of President Theodore Roosevelt.

Blighty had once killed a mountain lion that had attacked him and had helped to solve the murder of a man who had been his companion for many years. Butt was very proud of Blighty because he was his great great great Grandfather. Every time Blighty was mentioned Butt gave out a rusty sounding eeaawww and smiled.

Everyone did their scorpion checks, covered their boots with their socks then settled down to sleep. Willie cuddled up to Butt next to the fire, and Jane slept next to the other women because it was nice to have some female company.

The night was black and the stars were like diamonds, there were millions of them, the sound of the water lulled Willie to sleep as his head moved up and down on Butts warm belly as he breathed contently.

The next morning the River Guides woke the group early with the smell of breakfast and fresh coffee, everyone had moonshine heads but could not let the River Guides know, so struggled to act normal. As Willie rolled over to stretch out he came face to face with a furry, snoring and very content creature. It looked very cute and he did not want to disturb it. It was in a deep peaceful sleep.

One of the River Guides had seen the animal and told Willie not to move; he promptly put a net over the creature and placed it into one of the wooden boxes, like the one Vicious Vicky had been put in to. The Guide explained that it was a Bobcat and they would let it go before they left in case it bit someone. Willie was very upset, he didn't think the Bobcat should be in the box, it had every opportunity to bite someone while they were asleep but didn't, it just curled up next to Willie and Butt and slept.

The poor cat cried like a baby in the box, it sounded pitiful and everyone felt so sorry for it. Willie told the Guide that they would be leaving camp after the group so they would let the Bobcat go, the Guide was not too happy about that idea, but Willie insisted so finally the Guide agreed. They waved the group off as they continued through the Canyon; Willie went to the box and opened it slowly. The Bobcat looked at Willie with big sad eyes and let out a small pitiful meow, it was so cute.

Willie took the box to the bushes and left it there so the Bobcat could make his own way out when he was ready. He watched from a distance and the cat eventually climbed out of the box and sniffed around. Willie expected to see the cat disappear into the bushes but it sat in front of the box looked at Willie and cried. It was very small for a Bobcat and also very timid; it was probably quite young and hadn't yet developed a fear of others.

Willie walked over to the cat and it rubbed up against his leg and purred. He took out some beef jerky from his pocket and held it out in front of the cat's nose; it gently took the meat and chewed on it. Willie didn't want to leave the cat behind but knew he had to.

Jane came over to see Willie and told him that she had found something while she was having a wee in the bushes. She had discovered the body of a female Bobcat. It looked like this poor little Bobcat was an orphan kitten. Willie was moved to tears and realised he could not leave this poor little mite on its own to become pray for bigger animals, that was why it had cuddled up to him and Butt, his mothers cold body held no protection for him.

Jane gathered up some dry grass and placed it into the box, she found some cloth on the raft and placed that inside too, she picked up the little kitten and stroked it gently, it snuggled into her looking for warmth and comfort. Jane decided to call the kitten Baby and she placed it into the box and it curled up in to a ball. They placed the box inside the storage compartment so that it was nice and dark and the kitten would not be afraid.

Jane worried about the kitten it must have been a while since it had had milk from its mother, they had dried milk with them for the biscuits so Jane mixed some bottled water with it, the water was warmed due to the temperature in the Canyon so it was just right for the kitten. She took an empty moonshine bottle, made a hole in the cork, and fed the kitten. It lapped it up finishing the whole lot in minutes. Jane lifted it out of the box and cuddled it while they floated down the river.

The raft was peaceful, Butt sat at the front dozing in the sunshine, Willie wrote in his journal, Jane sang softly to Baby the kitten as the river gently lapped them forwards.

They were slowly approaching Havasu Creek and the beauty which it encased. The Havasupai Indians, or blue water people, are American Indians who have made their home mainly in Cataract Canyon which leads to Havasu Creek for the past 800 years. The Havasupai speak their native language of Yuman.

In 1882, the tribe was forced to abandon all but 518 acres of their ancestral land to the Federal Government. Their fertile land was destroyed by the construction of the Santé Fe rail road. They were also victims of their land being misused and unlawfully entered due to The National Park Service. They fought for a century utilising the United States Judicial system to regain the land which was their ancestral right and finally succeeded in 1975 and regained 251,000 acres with the passage of the Congressional Bill, S.1296.

Their land consists of beautiful richly coloured waterfalls these have now become a tourist attraction which is a source of income to the Havasupai in order for them to survive in the modern world. All who visit the area are in awe of its beauty.

Willie, Jane, Baby and Butt arrived at Havasu Creek about midday the day before Ichee's memorial was to take place. They were going to hike the Hualapai trail to Beaver Creek. They stopped for lunch first and Jane made another bottle of milk for Baby. They had a good meal and plenty of coffee before mooring the raft and setting off. Jane carried baby, she made a type of sling for him to be carried on the front of her body so that her arms were free to use, Butt carried the supplies they needed and Willie led the way.

The hike would take a good few hours to Havasu Falls but Beaver falls was the first set of waterfalls they would come across, so if they stayed near Beaver Falls over night they would be there for the memorial in the morning.

It was very hot and the trail was dusty and rocky, they passed lots of hikers on the way. They stopped frequently to drink water and Jane fed Baby. After a few hours they arrived at Moony Falls. The falls were beautiful; the colour of the blue, green waters was breath taking against the rock colours. For a moment they just stood and looked without saying a word. It was so peaceful although there were other people there. Everyone was quiet because they were looking at the beauty in front of their eyes.

After spending some time at the falls cooling down and resting, they headed towards a nearby camp for the evening. Jane started to cook while Willie looked after Baby and un packed what they needed for the night. Baby was very inquisitive but never wandered far from them. Willie lifted him up to give him a cuddle and Baby pissed all over him, the way in which it came out confirmed that he was a he and everyone fell about laughing.

When they sat around the fire that evening, they were joined by a few hikers who were heading like most people, down to the Colorado in the opposite direction to Willie and his companions. It was always a pleasure to meet so many different an interesting people and share their stories.

They rehearsed the songs they were going to sing for Ichee's memorial and wound together some twigs which they found along the trail to create a woven wreath. In the middle of the wreath they tied an empty bottle of moonshine which swung back and forth, a fitting tribute without a doubt.

Jane settled Baby down to sleep on a blanket; he was quite happy to snuggle up in a ball and obviously had no intention of wandering off. Willie and Butt sat next to the fire for a while chewing on beef jerky and washing it down with coffee as Butt tipped some moonshine into his mug he felt a great love for Wille, he was moved to tears about the thought of having such a special friend. Butt knew that when Willie finished rafting down the Canyon, he would leave to follow more adventure and he would miss him very much.

Finally they both fell asleep next to the fire which took the chill off the desert night air and sent orange sparks into the black inky sky. The Canyon was very eerie at night because it was so huge, dark and cold; the noises there were not like any which would be heard anywhere else. Being a mile down into the earth inside an inverted mountain could be a very strange feeling but one which was unique and awe inspiring, it is a world inside a world.

The morning was again beautiful, with the sun rising and lighting up the Canyon and revealing the palate of colours neatly layered in the walls. The rays of sun slowly and gently stretched as far as they could into every reachable part of the Canyon.

Baby woke first because he was very hungry and was crying around Jane's sleeping bag. She got up and made him up a bottle of milk, and put on some fresh coffee. They were not sure what time everyone would be at the memorial but as it was planned for 14.00 hours they thought that most people would be travelling from dawn if they were coming from the rim.

When they had eaten and the coffee was finished, they packed up and started to walk to Beaver Falls. To access Beaver falls, they would have to go past Moony falls and then go back on themselves for four miles, because the only way to enter Beaver Falls is through Moony Falls. It was a long hot walk but they passed the time by singing. On the double back walk from Moony Falls to Beaver Falls, they met up with some of Ichee's family and a Ranger named Bill who was guiding them to the memorial.

They had to cross a few creeks which were waste deep and then descend down a rope to get into Beaver Falls. Willie went down the rope first so that he could help Jane down with Baby. Once he and Jane were down, Ichee's brothers and sisters made their way down. Soon there was just Butt and Ranger Bill left to descend the rope. Butt did get down defying all the laws of nature and looking hysterically funny.

The only way he could to it was by wrapping his front hooves around the rope and getting them tied together, then wrapping his hind hooves around the rope and getting those tied together, which Ranger Bill helped him with. To lower himself down the rope and control the speed he would use his teeth as breaks. Considering he was a large animal and not as graceful as most, he did manage to make the decent into Beaver Creek without incident. Although no one wanted to stand underneath him as he clenched his way down the rope.

Everyone was relieved when he reached the bottom, but had no idea how he was going to get out later. Most of Ichee's family were there but it was difficult to see if any of them bore any resemblance to him. Each of them was wearing a disguise because they had entered the country illegally and were wanted in Canada.

Beaver Falls was truly beautiful. The green, blue waters caught up in a series of pools which cascaded into each other, some people say that because of these cascading pools Beaver Falls is not really a water fall at all, but did it really matter when the sight before you was so awesome.

Jane and Willie prepared the memorial, with the help of Ranger Bill. They tied the wreath to a nearby cotton wood tree and poured out water for everyone. Willie asked if any of Ichee's friends or family would like to say something at the service. A very petite Beaver walked up to Willie and said that she would like to throw some petals into the pools of water when the time was right, she said her name was Becci and she had secretly loved Ichee but found his foul mouth extremely off putting.

Willie was very glad that Becci had made it to the memorial and told her that Ichee had been very fond of her and had talked about her a lot and that his foul mouth had been cured.

Becci seemed moved to tears and became very emotional, Jane went up to her and gave her a hug. At 2pm everyone gathered around the bottom pool and Willie stood to the front on a rock and made a very moving speech. He told everyone about the short but memorable time which they had spent together and how quickly Ichee became part of their expedition and the wonderful company he was, how he had a zest for life and had made them all laugh.

The atmosphere was very solemn and all heads were bowed to the floor. Becci walked forward and gently sprinkled her petals into the pool. She stepped back and by this time everyone was in floods of tears as they all recalled their own personal memories of Ichee.

Jane stood forward from the mourners and started to sing one of Ichee's favourite Lionel Richie songs.

"I've been alone with you inside my mind

And in my dreams I've kissed your lips a thousand times

I sometimes see you pass outside my door . . . ."

Just at that moment the song was interrupted by something coming towards them on a rope, it was brown and furry and it sang out

"Hello is it me your looking for" everyone stared in disbelief, it was Ichee, he was alive and approaching at great speed with his toothy white grin spreading from one ear to the other. As they looked on in surprise and with great emotion at their pal's return from the dead, some of them suddenly realised he probably had no means of stopping and jumped into the pool followed by everyone else.

Ichee lowered himself down the rope as he flew through the air and in doing so managed to slow down the swinging process, once he had almost reached the bottom he let go and landed in the empty pool above everyone else.

"Wow" he said

"A pool party wicked"

Willie stood up in the water and didn't know whether to punch Ichee or hug him everyone was stunned and just stood in silence.

Jane walked out of the water, went over to her bag and handed everyone a drink of water. Ichee was not sure but he thought he could sense a slight atmosphere around the pools but he just stood and gave them his best smile. Willie went up to Ichee and gave him a huge hug he was so glad to see his friend again.

CHAPTER ELEVEN

Everyone stood and stared at Ichee, they couldn't believe what they were seeing. Becci was crying and throwing up behind a tree. Jane stood open mouthed. All of his brothers and sisters dropped their disguises, they could not compete with the impact Ichee had just made. Butt was so excited he eeeawed loudly, cracked open a bottle of moonshine and downed it all in one. It looked like Ichee had some explaining to do, no one was angry with him they were just overjoyed to see him. He obviously had a story to tell and there were at least twenty five pairs of ears who wanted to hear it.

Ichee sat down and everyone formed a semi circle around him to hear what he had to say. He went back to the day they were at Crystal Rapid. He told them that when he was on the raft he was enjoying the rapid right up until the raft had gone vertical and he had been hanging by the ropes, his mouth went into involuntary biting spasms due to pure fear. When he was sliding down the raft, he tried so very hard to avoid Butt and when he had been launched into the air he had flown a few yards and then landed in an eddy at the edge of the rapid. He was sent swirling around and around at speed.

Because of his life jacket he didn't sink but eventually passed out and was unconscious for a few hours. That was why no one could see him and he couldn't hear anyone calling him.

The next thing he knew he was opening his eyes and starring up at the Canyon walls from a beach. A hiker had seen him in the eddy and had pulled him out. Thinking he was dead he left Ichee on the beach alone.

Ichee felt very lucky to be alive but he was totally lost without his friends and had nothing to eat or drink. He wandered around in the heat for hours and eventually a river running group came across him and gave him food, water and first aid treatment. He hiked up the Canyon during the dark because he could not stand the heat in the day time, during the day he stayed close to the walls to keep out of the sun. He did this because he had suffered a slight fracture to his skull and the sun triggered severe migraines.

When he reached the plateau he thought he would hike to Peach Springs which was a small town and the starting point for many who were hiking to Havasu falls. Ichee knew that he would be able to catch up with Willie, Jane and Butt when he got there. He had followed them for a little while with the intention of surprising them.

Surprise them he did and he was also surprised because he had no idea that he was landing in the middle of his memorial and was even more surprised at how many people loved him enough to go to the trouble of doing something so wonderful. He was truly moved.

Everyone sat and listened to Ichee and tears rolled down their faces. No one could speak as the emotion was so high. Becci sat quietly on her own, she had not told Ichee how she felt, and had no idea how he would react to her after she had shunned him for using foul language.

Ichee noticed Becci sitting alone and his heart jumped for joy. He realised that he could not let this second chance with her get away; he had lost her once and had no intention of doing so again. Life, he had recently learned was too short not to fight for what you wanted.

He walked up to Becci opened his mouth and sang beautifully to her, he continued to sing "Hello" but this time he finished the whole song. As he sang the last few words he knelt down in front of her took her paw into his and looked lovingly into her eyes. The tears in Becci's eyes turned from sad ones to happy ones and she smiled beautifully. He leaned towards her and gently kissed her.

Everyone cheered for them both they made a lovely couple. Ichee told her that Jane had cured him from his foul word affliction and that he would never use such words again. In fact he was going to enrol in a night school class so that he could learn English correctly and write wonderful stories and poems. His near death experience had brought on a completely new meaning to his life he knew what was important to him now.

After a couple of hours it was time to move on from Beaver Falls, they would have to climb back up the rope again and head back towards Moony Falls. They would make a camp between the two falls that night.

The problem they were now faced with was how to get Butt up the rope. Not only was he going against gravity, but he had also drunk a bottle of moonshine to himself and had not added one drop of coffee to it. As challenges went this was a good one.

Ranger Bill suggested they got everyone else up first and Willie stayed at the bottom to help Butt up. He had a good strong net in his back pack and if Butt could curl up small enough to fit into it they could tie the net to the rope and pull him up. It would be very important for Butt to keep still and not wriggle about.

One by one everyone climbed out of Beaver Falls. Baby who had slept through the whole drama of the day was still strapped to Jane, and did not stir. When Ranger Bill reached the top and everyone was settled he sent down the net for Butt. Willie decided it would be a good idea if he went into the net with Butt to make sure he kept still.

As everyone at the top pulled with all their might to haul the net up Butt started to giggle, this turned into a chuckle and then a full blown laugh. He was very drunk and suddenly to the misfortune of everyone else started to recall the funny sight of Ichee flying through the air singing "Hello"

His laughter became uncontrollable and could not have happened at a worse time. Willie slid down further into the net because Butt was rolling about and he ended up being wedged against the net and Butts arse. Willie yelled for them to pull the net up faster, they tried their best to do so but because Butt was moving about in hysterical drunken laughter they struggled. The net was getting very heavy.

Willie was sure they were going to be dropped to the ground. He pleaded with Butt to stop laughing, and eventually he managed to wriggle out of his crushing position and climbed on to Butts head. He told Butt quite firmly that if he didn't stop laughing and putting their lives in danger he would not be allowed to continue down the Canyon on the raft.

Thankfully that worked and Butt stopped laughing. They managed to pull the net up and they were all reunited at the top. Willie got out of the net and Butt climbed out sheepishly after him. He knew he was in the dog house and would have to do something pretty cool to make up for it.

Butt was loaded up with their belongings once again and did offer to carry Jane and Baby, but Jane said she would not trust him to carry anything else until he could walk in a straight line. Ichee asked Becci if she would like to stay with the group or if she would prefer to go home, she said she would love to see Havasu Falls so would like to stay with the group.

It was getting dark and slightly cold so as soon as they were able they set up their camp. Ranger Bill told them that the waterfalls here were his favourite but in 2008; a storm had caused a flash flood and completely wiped out Navajo falls which was devastating as the falls were beautiful. It was a reminder to people that it was the force of nature which had shaped and created the Canyon to what people see today.

Smaller waterfalls were created by the destruction of Navajo falls which is a perfect example of how things can change even without man having a hand in it. The new waterfalls were just as lovely because anything created or changed by nature is to be looked upon in awe.

Ranger Bill was very interesting to talk to he had worked in that part of the Canyon for many years. He was very well liked and trusted by the native Havasupai people.

During the night there was a terrific thunder storm on the North Rim which could be seen from where they were camped. Ranger Bill told them that if it started to rain they would have to leave camp and head towards the Havasupai Village and possibly out of the Canyon because of the threat of a flash flood. They hoped very much it wouldn't rain because they didn't want to leave their cosy camp.

They sat and watched the storm it was amazing, each time the lightening lit up the sky the colours of the Canyon walls were awoken providing a spectacular scene for anyone who was watching. The sky looked angry and full of power, the thunder roared and found its way through the Canyon and every contributory canyon it could find. Every so often a crooked finger of bright white reached out and touched the Canyon walls sending bolts of electricity down through its geological structures.

Nature could be angry at times but when she let out a storm like this in a place like this, she was beautiful. As the storm grew quieter and moved away, they all slowly started to drift off to sleep, the threat of flooding had gone and Ranger Bill was content that they were all safe and sound for the night.

When the morning sun arrived, they woke one by one and helped themselves to coffee which Ranger Bill had made. They would today reach Havasu Falls and see one of the most beautiful sights in the Grand Canyon. Ichee was unnaturally quiet, and it did not go un noticed. Jane asked him if he was alright and he told her that he really loved Becci and wanted to marry her but was afraid that she would turn him down. Jane advised him that he should ask her, but not in front of everyone else because it should be a private moment between them.

Later that day Jane saw Ichee and Becci sitting quietly together and wondered if he was proposing to her, she walked on to give them their privacy. Butt was sober at last so Jane trusted him to carry Baby for a while because he was getting very heavy. Baby was drinking six bottles of milk every day and Jane knew that he should soon be on a solid diet.

Baby's sling was tied to Butt so he could not fall off and he sat contently on his back as they walked along the trail. Eventually they reached Havasu Falls. Ranger Bill told them that they would witness something very special and he was not wrong. The falls were truly beautiful from high in the red rock the blue, green water poured out and splashed into the natural pool below. The colours were amazing. Surrounding the pool was an array of rich green colour provided by trees and bushes. It was an oasis of life which could only be described as one of nature's greatest achievements.

The water was so inviting, there were other people bathing in the waters so some of the group including Ranger Bill decided to join them. Ichee and Becci stood on the edge of the pool gazing into each other's eyes with deep contentment; all that existed from their point of view was each other and Havasu Falls.

When Ranger Bill came out of the water, Ichee approached him and told him that Becci had accepted his marriage proposal and they could not think of a better place to get married than right there at Havasu Falls. Ranger Bill told them that he could perform the ceremony for them if they would like him to. They were very excited, they told everyone about the plan and they all hurried around getting ready planning a lovely ceremony for them.

Jane gathered some wild flowers to put in Becci's fir and Willie gathered all the drink he could find mostly water and moonshine. Within an hour everything was ready. Everyone stood around the pool and Ichee and Becci stood with Ranger Bill on a rock beside the waterfall, they both made their vows and everyone cheered they thought it was wonderful. Ichee picked Becci up in his arms and carried her through the water to the shore. He sat her down on a log and serenaded her with

"Three times a Lady"

They stayed at the falls and partied for a few hours, Ichee's brothers were given some moonshine but Jane was in charge of alcohol so they didn't have as much as they would have liked. They complained about the luke warm water so Willie gave them some mints to suck on before they drank it like the cowboys used to do.

Willie started to dance and everyone joined in, they kicked their heels and linked arms as they swung each other around. By night fall they were all so exhausted that Ranger Bill thought it would be best if they camped where they were.

The next morning, there was word that the authorities were looking for Ichee's brothers and sisters. Ranger Bill told them that they should give themselves up then they could stop running. Giving up being wanted was not an option because they enjoyed it so much, it was fun. When everyone was walking on the trail, they diverted and went another way. When Ichee turned around to speak to one of his brothers, they were all gone. Ichee was sad but he smiled to himself because having a family who were fugitives was quite exciting.

Willie found all of this very amusing but by this time he really wanted to be river running again. His raft was ready and waiting and he wanted to be on it challenging the river and himself. When they sat down for a rest, Wille asked who was going to continue on the raft with him.

Butt said that he could not wait to get back on the raft, but Ichee said he and Becci wanted to go and find themselves a home. Willie completely understood and told them that he would miss them both very much. Jane told Willie that she thought it was time she went to collect Floating Cloud and went back to see Ma Cahill because she had been on her own for a few weeks now.

Ranger Bill arranged for Floating Cloud to be taken to The El Tovar Hotel so Jane could save time, she would also take Baby with her. Willie would miss Jane but knew that she had to go home and had work to do at the Navajo reservation.

So it was just Willie and Butt, the two pals together again to start the final part of their journey to mile 277 Pearce Ferry, Lake Mead. After some tearful goodbyes the group parted company and went their separate ways. Willie and Butt reached the raft by early evening and set up camp for the night.

The next morning they woke early and had a good breakfast and a good fill of coffee. They wanted to do a whole day on the Colorado so they could make up for lost time.

CHAPTER TWELVE

While they were drifting along they could hear a lot of singing, shouting and laughing. Wille turned back and saw a river running group behind them. It was obvious from first sight that they were not an official guided group. There were seven young men and they were all drinking alcohol and smoking.

They drifted past Willie and Butt, one of the men said

"Hey dudes look at this a raft with a biscuit and a donkey on it"

Butt hated being called a donkey and was not amused. Willie thought they were very rude and silly. He also knew that the word "Dude" was a name given to city folk who never left the city and these guys were not wearing suits and they were not in the city so why were they calling each other "Dude" they were obviously ignorant too.

Unless it came out of a book Willie could not comprehend it. He didn't know that some words over time evolve into some other meaning than their original use, mainly because they are used as slang.

The group had annoyed Butt and he really had his back up over it. Willie was just confused these guys were behaving in the most peculiar way and they didn't seem to be taking the Colorado seriously. Butt had seen their type before they spend a few weeks down the Canyon getting through on pure luck, strange smelling cigarettes and cheap alcohol. They party all the time dancing from dusk till dawn then back on the river.

Butt was not as naive as Willie, the old timer had told him about certain things people did to enhance their natural high. He told Willie that "Dude" was a word which was used as a term of greeting people in this day, sort of cool. Willie still looked puzzled. He explained again, that it was more like a laid back way of speaking to someone or greeting them, it was not seen as rude and it was ok for him to call people dude if they used the word themselves.

Willie just accepted what Butt said. He thought that he had a lot to learn about the modern world. Books were fantastic, but it appeared they supplied the theory of life and not the practicality of it. He decided that was a very important point for him to remember.

The dudes on the raft drifted past them, they were very loud but they were having a fantastic time. Once they had gone the rest of the afternoon was very pleasant, the river was very calm and they drifted along peacefully. They both felt lazy and thought they would set up camp at the next beach and lay on the sand for a while and

"Chill out" as Butt described it.

As they approached the shore they were delighted to see another river running group had already set up a camp. Willie was beginning to enjoy the company of others as their stories and experiences enriched his knowledge of the Canyon and were truly inspirational. If they were nice they may ask them to join them and then they wouldn't have to set up their own camp.

As they got closer and moored the raft, they realised that the group were the dudes from the raft earlier that day. Butt was not happy because they had called him a donkey, but they waved to them beckoned them over and asked them if they wanted to join their camp.

Butt told Willie that it would be nice to join them but he wanted them to be certain that he was a mule and not a donkey.

Willie thanked them for their offer, he introduced himself, and he introduced Butt as a mule so there were no further misunderstandings. They asked him how come he was a biscuit and was walking and talking. He explained to them that it was a complete fluke and that his dough had been contaminated by human DNA. He does not get wet because he has been varnished so it keeps him water tight.

"Cool you still smell good though dude, I can smell the ginger from here" one of the dudes remarked. Willie smiled and took it as a compliment.

These dudes were definitely up for a good time and they had adventure running through their veins. They sat and re lived a rapid which they had run that day which they described as

"Total carnage"

Willie was fascinated by the way they seemed to accept adventure with no fear of the unknown, he admired that quality because he could see it in himself and he knew at that point that the passion he felt inside for adventure truly was a human feeling which could only have been produced by the DNA in his blood.

They used a lot of words which Willie didn't understand, Butt told him they were words people used when running rivers, and it was called river terminology.

The dudes asked Willie if they had any "Stuff" Willie said that they had loads and it was all stashed on the raft. He said they could help themselves to whatever they wanted pointing to the food supplies. One of the dudes told Willie it was very kind of him and he really shouldn't share his "stuff" with just anyone. Willie assured him it was fine he had been told by Ma Cahill to share whatever he had with others; it was old fashioned good manners.

He told the dude to go into the storage compartment on the left of the raft and he would find what he needed. He did this and searched around for a while. He returned to the camp fire looking confused and defeated. Butt asked Willie what the dude was doing rooting through the raft. Willie told him he was looking for stuff and he had told them they could have whatever they needed.

Butt realised Willie had no idea what the dudes were referring to as "stuff" so he went to the raft and told them that they had no "stuff" left. They did have some nice clear alcohol however which he thought they would enjoy very much. Butt took out a bottle of moonshine and winked at Willie as he passed it around the group. When they had all had a few mouthfuls, Butt leaned over to Willie and explained to him the real meaning of "stuff" Willie was rather miffed but was interested to see what would unfold from the dudes drinking the moonshine.

They all sat in a circle around the fire and soon the bottle was empty, one of the guys was going to get up and get another bottle but Butt immediately jumped up and went to get another bottle for them. They took the second bottle and passed it around the camp. Butt was laughing to himself because he knew that as long as they sat drinking they would not feel the full effects but as soon as they stood up it would hit them like a bolder being carried by a flash Canyon flood.

Although there was food cooking over the fire, they were too interested in the bottle of moonshine to eat. Butt told Willie that they were going to have to stay awake because the form of entertainment which was about to take place was worth buying tickets for and they had a front row seat for free.

One of the dudes eventually needed to go to the river for a pee, his friend next to him decided to join him and they quickly stood up to go. Until that moment they had not felt a thing but as soon as their feet touched the sand, it hit them. The moonshine which had a kick like a mule turned their legs into spaghetti. Their upper body was too heavy for their spaghetti legs and they buckled under the weight. They tried to hold onto something but there was nothing but inky air. They grabbed hold of each other and both fell to the floor with a thud.

The rest of the group got up and looked over to see them laying on the sand, then like a very well organised domino drop one by one they fell and knocked over the next one in line. They all rolled about on the floor spaghetti legs stretched out all over the place. Some of the dudes were actually crying and some were just lying there, the one who had searched the raft kept repeating

"That's some shit dude"

Butt fell about laughing, he knew they were used to smoking "Stuff" because the old timer he used to hang about with smoked it all the time to help with his arthritis. What these dudes didn't know was that bootleg moonshine was guaranteed to do this every time unless you were really hardened to the stuff. Willie was a bit cross with Butt and told him he should not have let them drink so much and encouraged them. He got up and put a pot of fresh coffee and some biscuits on the fire to try and soak up some of the alcohol in their stomachs.

Because Butt was feeling mischievous, he decided that Willie was being a bit stuffy and he really should lighten up and have a laugh. Butt had a good drink of the moonshine and a good few spoonfuls of warm beans from the fire, he shoved it all down quickly to create pockets of wind in his digestive system. When he was finished, he borrowed a harmonica from one of the dudes which was lying on a sleeping bag. He told Willie that he had a really good trick to show them all while they were having their coffee and biscuits. He waited for them to at least be able to sit upright and then said he was ready to perform.

He put the harmonica in his mouth and wrapped his gums around it. Then he knelt down on his front legs with his backside in the air and aiming at the fire. He started to play duelling banjos on the harmonica he was very good, everyone wondered what he was going to use for the second instrument. They didn't have to wonder for too long however because when it was time for the second instrument to join in Butts arse let out a series of farts which mimicked the notes on the harmonica.

As each fart reached the fire it set alight it was like a musical fire work display, the flames went blue indicating a good moonshine and everyone fell about laughing. Butt played the tune faster and faster, flames shooting out of his arse and his gums flapping over the harmonica. He loved it and the more they laughed the faster he "played" there was nothing he liked more than a captive audience.

Willie who had first sat and looked on in disbelief was now rolling about on the sand unable to breathe he was laughing so much. He had never seen anything so funny. The dudes clapped to the music encouraging him to play even faster and the farts shot out like gun shots over the Canyon.

By the time it came to the end of the music everyone was crumpled up on the floor with laughter trying to stop themselves from pissing their pants because their legs were still too wobbly to walk to the river for a pee. Butt stood up and bowed to his audience, but although he was able to stop playing the harmonica he unfortunately had no control over his rear end for quite some time. It took a long time for everyone to go to sleep because the image they had witnessed was so funny they couldn't stop laughing. Eventually the moonshine acted as an anaesthetic and they drifted off to sleep one by one.

The next morning everyone was laying still they couldn't move. The dudes just lay on the sand groaning. Willie went around giving them all fresh coffee and pancakes he made them as comfortable as he could. The only thing they could do was sleep it off. One by one they managed to get up to answer the call of nature and although their legs were now working, they had not regained their balance or sense of direction and they staggered towards the Colorado.

The leader of the group who had searched for the "Stuff" was Mikey, he told Butt and Willie that he had never been so totally wasted and wanted to know what he had been given to drink. Willie explained that it was bootleg moonshine and that they were not to tell anyone about it.

Mikey said that the secret was safe with them, because of the alcohol the previous evening and the entertainment they had not all been properly introduced. The six of his friends were Richie, Donny,

Jamie, Jack, Pete, and Chris they were all from California and this adventure had blown them away. Willie told them that it had been a really memorable evening for many reasons and he hoped they all enjoyed the rest of their Canyon adventure. It did feel good making new friends especially ones who enjoyed the Canyon as much as they did. Willie and Butt said thank you to the dudes for their company and headed for the raft.

The dudes were not ready to get back on the river just yet they thought the motion of the water may cause mass nausea so planned a day and another night at that spot.

When Willie and Butt got back to the raft, he had the shock of his life, sitting as bold as brass at the front of the raft with a face so expressionless it could have been made of stone was Fanny. She turned abruptly to Willie and told him she was accompanying him to Separation Canyon as she had business to attend to there and would appreciate it if he kept things as quiet and as still as possible.

Willie and Butt were stunned. Although Butt had not met her before, he shivered from head to foot at the mere sight of her hard, cold presence. Butt looked at Willie and the whites of his eyes revealed sheer terror, Willie patted him on the back to reassure him and gave him a smile. He told Butt that Separation Canyon was not too far down river so she would not be with them for long.

Willie was curious about the business which Fanny said she had to attend to but knew he was better off not knowing he just hoped it wasn't evil.

As they floated along with a little help from the oars, Butt felt rather put out as Fanny was sitting at the front of the raft and that was his place. Every time he moved towards the front she glared at him with a look of pure evil, so he shrank backwards and settled for sitting in the middle.

Soon they were to hit the first rapid with Fanny on board and this was 232 rapid which is said to be the one which sealed the fate of Glen and Bessie Hyde the Canyon honeymoon couple. Willie told Fanny she should hold onto the ropes as it was a very dangerous and unpredictable rapid with rocks which protruded out of the water described as killer "fangs"

The cfs (cubic feet per second)of the water was pretty good and in their favour, the rapid usually was described as being 4-7, Willie estimated that it would possible be about a 5 this however did mean that the fangs could be difficult to see within the rapid.

Fanny completely shunned the advice given and sat upright at the front of the raft. Butt had no choice than to hook his hooves into the side ropes where Jane had been and Willie again took his position at the raised platform to enable him to scout the rapid as best he could from the raft.

The noise as usual came first, Willie braced himself and told Fanny and Butt that 232 was looking rowdy and that the run would be pretty sick, he had learned this terminology from the dudes. Butt responded by checking his ropes were tight. Then they hit. The raft was thrown into full animation, twisting, turning, up and down. Willie was only interested in avoiding the fangs; he knew that anything beyond control of that was wishful thinking. As they rocked and spun about Willie looked to see if Butt was alright, he was holding on for his life, but as always had a huge grin on his face.

Willie looked at Fanny, she remained on the front of the raft in the same position as she had been before the rapid, it was as though she had an iron rod through her body impaling her in position. She did not move she did not flinch. As much as this troubled Willie ahead he could just about make out the fangs in the white frothing water, so took hold of his oars and began to prepare to negotiate around them.

He struggled, the water wanted him to go towards the Fangs and he had a real battle on his hands, he told Butt to untie himself and grab one of the oars so he could help. Butt did and they both had a mammoth battle with the rapid. Water was thrown all over them and the raft, they went vertical in both directions and at one time almost flipped the raft over, this rapid was awesome but Willie did not think they were going to make it through.

Due to luck or skill they managed to pass the Fangs, but they were still not out of danger. When they past the Fangs, they had been quite vertical at the rear, the raft slapped back down onto the water with a mighty bang and hit another rock which was partially visible within the white wash.

Willie was thrown forward and grabbed hold of Butt, he managed to stay on the raft but part of the rear had been damaged revealing a hole which was now letting in water. Searching around desperately to find something to plug the hole with Willie grabbed a piece of cloth and rammed it in. It seemed to hold off the water for a while but he knew it would not be for long and they really would need to pull into the shore very soon.

The rapid thankfully started to subside, the froth started to calm down and the white water unwillingly gave way to the calmer water. Willie took the other oar from Butt and rowed toward the river edge to take refuge on the sandy shore.

They both got off the raft and pulled it onto the sand while Fanny still sat in pole position at the front. Willie and Butt lay on the sand exhausted and looked into the sky. Glad to be alive they both turned and looked at each other and said

"Total Carnage Dude"

Fanny remained where she was. Willie told her that they would be moving on as soon as he had repaired the raft and he would make some coffee to warm them up. She did not move, just sat in the same position and stared ahead.

Butt looked at her and could not help but laugh. He had held it in all this time but now could no longer see the point. He blurted out his crude sounding but hysterically funny belly laugh she was so weird that only laughter would do at this point. Fanny didn't say a word, she simply turned her head in Butt's direction very slowly and stared at him with so much evil in her eyes that he immediately stopped laughing and whimpered. She turned her head back to the forward position and didn't move again.

Willie asked Butt to look around to see if he could find some wood to repair the raft. Butt found some drift wood and took it back to Willie who had by this time made some coffee. They sat and relaxed totally in awe that they had conquered rapid 232. Fanny didn't drink coffee eat anything or even have a sip of water.

Willie took a good look at the damage on the raft, it wasn't too bad. If he removed the damaged piece of log and replaced it with the bit that Butt found it should be fine. He cut away the broken piece and then tied the replacement piece on riveting it together with strong rope. Soon they were ready to go and both got back onto the raft.

There were a few small rapids between 232 and Separation Canyon but they were easily passed and the raft seemed to hold well enough. Separation Canyon was on the North side of the Canyon and Willie wondered why Fanny would want to go there. He knew she was up to something, he didn't trust her at all. As they approached the end of Fanny's raft ride, Willie was very glad to be seeing the back of her. She had made the last thirty miles very unpleasant and uneasy.

Opposite Separation Canyon, he stopped and Fanny stood up from her position on the raft and walked off onto the sand, Willie had no idea how she was going to cross the river and at that point didn't care very much he was just glad she was gone.

He pushed the raft away from the shore and rowed forwards not looking back once. There was something so wrong with Fanny that he thought he would be turned to stone if he so much as turned back and looked at her. Butt was obviously relieved she was gone and assumed his position at the front of the raft, although he did give it a good wash down where she had been sitting in case there was any evil on that spot. Fanny had crossed the river by some means and was now heading for Separation Canyon.

In a small slot canyon tucked away, was a sinister figure waiting for her, he was surrounded by gingerbread dolls which were individually dressed and had hair or fur stuck on them. The one with the fur had been floating in a small pool of river water and represented Ichee. The sinister figure was the fugitive who had been at Ma Cahill's.

The next few miles were very relaxing, the sun was hot and the water was calm, it was another truly beautiful day in the Canyon. The walls were glimmering with colour, and the shores were full of people partying and enjoying the Canyon. They were almost at the end of the 277 miles of Colorado through the Grand Canyon. Although they had thoroughly enjoyed the rapids Willie did think that it would be nice if the last forty five miles were uneventful so they could enjoy the beauty the Canyon had to offer. He knew there were two more rapids which they could run, 234 rapid and Bridge Canyon Rapid at mile 235, these would have to be their final rapids of the Canyon, they would drift out in style.

There were two other rapids but they were not going to run those. Pearce Ferry rapid is not rated because it only formed in 2007 when Lake Mead fell below 1138 feet. This rapid would not be within the challenge as Major Powell had not run it. Pearce Ferry take out was not operational after 2009 because the elevation at the ramp is about 1150 and the elevation of Lake Mead was 1096.92 in May 2009 so they could not possibly go any further.

So they were left with the last two, 234 and 235 which were a good rating, more of a thrill to end the trip with rather than a white knuckle wee your pants ride. They floated along for forty miles chatting and laughing about the times they had enjoyed and the people they had met over the last few weeks.

CHAPTER THIRTEEN

Their final two rapids went well and they rode them with great fun and enthusiasm knowing they would be their last. They decided it would be nice to mark the end of their journey through the Grand Canyon. To everyone else they would be just another raft with river runners on board but to them the end of the expedition was a huge milestone in their lives.

They had come so far in many ways and had learnt so much. Their personalities had been changed by their experiences, the people they had met along the way and the friends they had made. Willie truly believed that doing what he had done had brought him closer to nature and its beauty and dangers. He had been in touch with his human side, and had felt many different emotions. The biggest lesson he had learned was that life was not in the form of a book, you had to live it.

Willie found a piece of white fabric in the first aid kit. He told Butt that they should draw something on it and wave it as a flag as they completed mile 277. After a little thought, they decided it would be nice to draw a picture of each other as they best remembered each other on the trip.

Butt took his turn first, when he had drawn Willie he rolled his part of the cloth up so Willie couldn't see what he had drawn while he drew his picture of Butt. While Willie was drawing Butt found a stick which they had used for mixing up the pancake mixture and thought that would be perfect for attaching to the fabric to turn it into a flag.

When Willie had finished, he and Butt sat in the middle of the raft and had an unveiling ceremony. When they opened the fabric they both fell about laughing. The pictures were fantastic and very funny. Butt had drawn Willie as the captain of the raft with Ichee on his shoulder in place of a parrot and his eyes as spirals resembling his first encounter with moonshine. Willie had drawn Butt from the rear view he had so often seen, with his head looking back at him, gums rolled back over his teeth, ears pinned back and his back side in the air as they rode a rapid.

They were both hysterical with laughter and opened a bottle of moonshine to get the party started. Willie insisted they ate with the moonshine because it would be such a shame to make it all that way and not remember the final few miles. He got out some biscuits and opened a tin of beans, they were very excited.

As they prepared for the final part of their journey Willie started to become rather nostalgic it would be such a pity for a wonderful adventure to come to an end. But then an adventure would not be an adventure if it didn't come to an end. The positive thought was he lived here so he could visit any time, but there would never be anything quite like this time.

The final miles were approaching. They were both in full swing. They has sensibly limited the amount of moonshine and eaten a good amount of food, but it was the excitement and the adrenaline which was causing the high spirits.

As the water miles disappeared under the raft the final approach was made, Wille and Butt had made it they had completed their trip and although sad to see it end, they felt a huge sense of achievement. At the official end which was as far as they could go they raised their flag to mark their arrival.

On the river bank there was a group of people cheering and shouting and waving their hands. Willie wondered what all the fuss was about but as they drew nearer he could see Jane, Ichee, Becci and a few of the river runners they had encountered on the way, they were all there to welcome and congratulate them.

With tears in their eyes and a sudden gust of wind behind them they drifted into the shore to a welcome anyone would be proud of. As they stepped off the raft they were both full of emotion, it was such a wonderful surprise to see everyone and it meant such a lot to them.

Jane had organised a wonderful spread of food which had been brought down to the Canyon by some of Butt's mule friends who he had not seen in a long time. Butt was truly moved, they were all so happy to see him especially as they had been able to make it down the Canyon without the fear of being bitten by Vicious Vicky.

The entertainment was provided by Ichee who had now learnt a few more songs and had ventured into some newer stuff. The whole beach rocked with atmosphere and everyone had a fantastic time.

Butt was so happy he felt so loved. Being the centre of attention really was his favourite pass time. He contemplated providing some entertainment himself in the form of the duelling banjo's he had demonstrated the previous night. When he mentioned the idea to Willie, he reminded him that there were ladies present and if he wanted to entertain people and make them laugh he should just be himself that was all he needed to do.

Of course the moonshine was being passed around, some of the mules to Butt's surprise declined the bootleg however, because they had become permanent trail mules and had the responsibility of carrying people down the Canyon. There had been few recorded accidents descending or ascending the Canyon on a mule and they wanted to keep it that way.

Exhausted from partying they all camped the night on the beach in the sleeping bags which Jane had carried down. This was to be Willie's last night in the Canyon for now until he returned again someday. He lay once again under the stars breathing in the scents and listening to the sounds he had become familiar with. He knew he would be back soon but he also knew that he had to explore other places too. When he returned home to Ma Cahill he would plan his next trip.

The next morning the sun didn't disappoint, it stretched out through the Canyon once again igniting the colours which it was blessed with. Everyone helped to pack up the camp. Willie was unsure what to do with the raft, he felt it belonged in the Canyon, but also wanted to take it home so he could use it when he returned another time. Jane told him to leave it where it was and they could collect it or arrange for it to be collected when they returned home. He pulled it onto the beach and Butt helped him to drag it into a nearby cave.

They took what they needed from the raft and left the beach to begin their journey to the rim. With the lack of a trail, it wasn't going to be easy, the best way was to head towards Lake Mead and then return to the rim from there. It was a difficult but enjoyable hike but the scenery was beautiful. Just before nightfall they reached the rim Jane had arranged a wagon and some mules to be waiting for them.

As Willie climbed onto the wagon Butt made a loud

"Eeeeeeeeeeeeoooooooooooooorrrrr" Willie wondered what was wrong with him and told him he could climb in the back if his legs were aching. Jane told Willie that Butt was trying to tell him something. Butt joined his friends and told Willie that he couldn't leave the Canyon he had to stay because it was his home and he knew no other.

Willie was distraught, he had not given a thought about Butt staying in the Canyon, and he just assumed he would travel home with him. Butt told Willie he would now find his way back to the place where they had first met because that was his part of the Canyon and that Willie would always know where to find him.

"Just light a fire and brew up the coffee and I won't be far behind you" he said.

With tears in his eyes Willie jumped down from the wagon and hugged Butt tightly. Without saying a word for fear of being choked with emotion, he got back onto the wagon. He looked behind him as the wagon started its journey back to Ma Cahill and he watched until Butt was out of sight and then turned and looked ahead.

As Butt made his way home he realised he had learned so much when he was with Willie, although he knew the Canyon well, he seldom made friends and joined in with Canyon users. He had seen the Canyon in a different way, not because he had been on a raft for the first time, but because he was seeing someone else's reaction to something he took for granted every day.

For the first hour of the journey Willie was very quiet, he knew he wasn't much company for Jane, but just couldn't bring himself to speak due to the emotion building up inside him. Jane knew how he was feeling so just drove the wagon letting Willie stay lost in his thoughts. He believed he had experienced a fantastic adventure, it had shaped him in many ways and he had felt many human emotions. This was the beginning of adventures for him and he wanted to do many more, he was not sure if he had changed in any way but it had made him even more thirsty for new challenges.

After two hours Jane and the mules needed a break so she stopped to feed and water them and make some coffee. Willie drank some coffee and it did make him feel a lot better, he had four sugars in it which bucked him up slightly. Jane told him that the friends he had made in the Canyon belonged in the Canyon and that he knew where they were when he needed them. She told him that Ichee and Becci had decided to set up home near Phantom Ranch because after leaving they quickly returned realising that they wanted to live their life in and around the Canyon. He began to cheer up a little and was encouraged by Jane to talk about the last few days.

He suddenly remembered about Fanny and the strange way she had appeared on the raft, he explained to Jane the weird way in which she did not move one millimetre when the raft was being tossed about violently at rapid 232. Jane looked horrified, it made her feel very uneasy that Fanny had been in the Canyon again, when she was at The El Tovar Hotel they knew where she was and felt safe. Now she was making her way up and down the Canyon she could be anywhere any time and planning anything.

They would be approaching Grand Canyon Village the next day and would call into The El Tovar Hotel to see why Fanny wasn't there. Jane was very worried and uneasy; even a day seemed too long to wait; Fanny could be up to anything.

The day of travelling seemed like a month; eventually they arrived at Grand Canyon Village and headed straight for the Hotel. When they arrived, the receptionist offered them refreshment immediately as it was obvious that they were both exhausted and in need of food and fluids. They sat down and she brought them some sandwiches and lemonade. As soon as Jane finished her refreshments she went outside to attend the mules.

Willie asked the girl about Fanny, the girl turned so pale Willie thought she was going to faint. Willie called Jane in from outside because he had a feeling she needed to hear what was coming next. The girl told them that her name was Emily and that she worked on reception most of the day, she said that about a week ago, she arrived at work to discover that two of her friends who worked in the kitchen, Eliza and Adam had been taken to hospital with serious injuries, both of them had been stabbed in the top of their leg.

At first it was thought they had been fighting with one another, they were a couple, but it was totally forbidden to argue and fight in the kitchen in case the guests over heard and anyone who did so would be dismissed immediately, they were planning getting married so losing their jobs would have been out of the question for them. Anyway who would be so incensed with someone they loved that they would stab them in the thigh a potentially fatal area. If it had not been for a guest sneaking into the kitchen unauthorised looking for food, they both would have been dead.

Willie dared to ask but he knew that he had to find out what this had to do with Fanny. Emily told them that Fanny was nowhere to be seen that day and that her room was left completely empty, it was as though she had never been there. The only trace of her was something the chef found in her locker in the kitchen. In the locker were two gingerbread people. They were beautifully made but it was very creepy because they both had human hair in them, this hair had un knowingly been cut from Eliza and Adam and in the top of the leg of each of them was a thick tapestry needle.

Willie felt so sick, he knew she was evil but what possible reason could Fanny have for doing this to two innocent young people. At that moment, the manager of the restaurant, Mr Jones walked into the hotel, he had been to visit Eliza and Adam, Emily was anxious for news of them. Willie introduced himself and Jane to Mr Jones, and explained that he had seen Fanny four days ago and she was heading for Separation Canyon.

Mr Jones told Willie that unfortunately they could not prove that Fanny had anything to do with the incident, because although the gingerbread dolls were very sinister, they themselves were not enough evidence to suggest that she had anything to do with it. The dolls could have been placed in the locker after the incident as everyone was busy attending to Eliza and Adam no one would have taken any notice of Fanny and what she was up to. It was still very creepy however that someone would want to mimic another's suffering in such a way.

Willie told Mr Jones that he and Jane were heading home and he could contact them if he needed to, leaving him the telephone number of the house. All the way home Willie and Jane felt uneasy, they knew Fanny had something to do with this, it was the third time she had used gingerbread dolls to bring harm to others for no apparent reason what sort of evil possessed her to do such a thing.

It was another four hours before they arrived home and they were exhausted, they knew that Ma Cahill would be pleased to see them and would immediately be in the kitchen preparing food and hot coffee for them. Jane couldn't wait to see her she had missed her so much and Ma Cahill had been looking after Baby for her while she was collecting Willie.

When the wagon drew up outside, Jane knew the mules had to be attended to first as they had had the hardest few days of all, she took them to the cattle shed and gave them fresh food and water. Baby was in the stall and lying very still, Jane went up to him expecting him to jump up when he saw her but he didn't. He just lay there, Jane picked him up in her arms and he was floppy and weak, she laid him on the straw and examined him quickly, his nose was very dry and his skin was loose, he was dehydrated.

She immediately got him some water and fed it to him in drips, Willie came into the cattle shed to see what Jane was doing, he could see her leaning over Baby crying and trying to get him to drink the drops of water.

He helped her by holding Baby while she opened his little mouth and poured drops of the water into his throat, slowly he began to move the muscles in his throat allowing the water to pass down into his tiny body.

It took a while but Baby did become a little more alert and opened his eyes, Jane was so relieved she hugged him and tears ran down her face onto his soft fur. He responded by licking her face. Soon afterwards, Baby was drinking water by himself to the relief of Jane and Willie. They had not been to the house yet and suddenly had a terrible fear, Ma Cahill would never have let Baby get into this condition, was she alright?

Willie told Jane not to go into the house; he would go in first to make sure that everything was alright. He opened the front porch door and walked into the house, he called for Ma Cahill but there was no answer, he slowly walked into the bedroom on his left, but she wasn't there, he walked into the lounge, but he couldn't see her. He walked towards the kitchen which meant he had to walk around the sofa, and on the floor in front of the television lay Ma Cahill she was very still and next to her was an empty bottle of moonshine.

Willie rushed to help her, but it was too late, it looked as though she had been there for some time, she was dead. Willie was so shocked he couldn't move, and then he remembered Jane was outside and did not want her to walk in and see this without being told first.

He picked himself up off the floor and somehow managed to walk his grief heavy body out to Jane. She took one look at Willie and knew that something was wrong, before he could open his mouth to tell her what he had found, she was already in the house and he could hear her painful wailing from outside. Jane held Ma Cahill in her arms and sobbed, she rocked back and forth asking why this could have happened. Willie went up to her and released Ma Cahill from Jane's arms. He sat Jane on a chair and covered Ma Cahill's body with a sheet from the bedroom, then telephoned the Sheriff.

Jane was shaking so much with the shock that Willie became very concerned about her. He went to the cattle shed and picked up Baby to take him to the house to comfort Jane. Once she had Baby, she seemed to calm a little so Willie thought he would go to the kitchen and make her a cup of tea which is supposed to be good for shock. No wonder poor Baby was dehydrated he must have been in the shed for at least two days without water in this heat.

When he entered the kitchen, Willie saw that everything was in its place as usual Ma Cahill always ran a tight ship. However in the corner of the kitchen near the window something was not right. He walked over to take a closer look, he was horrified. On the work top there was a glass bowl full of liquid, in the bowl was a gingerbread woman who was dressed just like Ma Cahill and some of Ma's hair had been pushed into the head which was now swollen with the liquid from the bowl.

It was truly a horrible sight which left Willie reeling with fear and shock, he opened the kitchen window for air but the Canyon air was hot and dry, the breath was taken from his body and he gasped to try and re claim it. Eventually he went to the sink and splashed his face with cold water jolting his body into taking in a breath which it desperately needed.

He knew the Sheriff would be here soon so he bravely went to the bowl to take out some of the liquid so he could test it, he did it very carefully so as not to disturb any vital forensic evidence, but he knew he had to test the liquid for himself. He made Jane some tea and took it to her; she was in the bathroom, so he took the opportunity to remove some of the tiny remains in the bottom of the bottle of moonshine next to Ma Cahill's body. He put the evidence he had collected into a container from the kitchen and into the fridge.

CHAPTER FOURTEEN

It was almost two hours before the Sheriff arrived; he had to come from Flagstaff and had been held up on the way. His four by four vehicle screeched up to the house and came to a sudden halt outside. The Sheriff was new and young, he had bountiful energy and enthusiasm, but somehow, Willie got the impression that he was lacking in the brains department.

Willie had learnt a few things from his friend Jon the policeman from the United Kingdom about Crime Preservation. He told the Sheriff who had introduced himself as Dwayne, that as far as he knew only he and Jane had been inside the house and they had done their best not to disturb too much just in case it was a crime scene.

Dwayne looked at Willie as though he were speaking a different language. He walked into the house, removed the sheet from Ma Cahill and took a good look at her.

"Looks like she went and got herself too much of the gin" he said.

Jane was about to tell Dwayne that it was moonshine but Willie gave her a glare to warn her to keep quiet, she realised Willie was onto something so agreed with Dwayne and told him that she did enjoy her gin.

The doctor came a while later and pronounced her dead he said the body would have to go to Flagstaff for an autopsy. Jane and Willie were very upset but they knew it had to be done. Willie was determined to get to the truth behind the death of Ma Cahill because he knew that she was a hardened moonshine drinker and only drank her own stuff or stuff given to her by friends who she trusted and had supplied her for years.

When Ma Cahill had been taken away, Jane went into the kitchen to make some coffee and something to eat. Willie walked up and down the steps outside desperately trying to make sense of the situation and find a clue in his mind. He had not shown Sheriff Dwayne the gingerbread lady dunked in the liquid, because he knew it wouldn't prove anything. It was obvious that Sheriff Dwayne didn't think the house was a crime scene. This was something which he would have to investigate himself.

Willie went into the kitchen because he realised he had not hidden the dunked gingerbread lady from Jane and it may freak her out. She had already seen it and hadn't been surprised or upset by it just angry. Willie told her that when they had eaten they would light up the moonshine he had retrieved from the bottom of the bottle beside Ma Cahill, light up some from Ma Cahill's stash, and some from the liquid containing the dunked gingerbread doll. He was sure Ma had been given bad moonshine.

That night Willie and Jane went through every clue which could prove that Fanny was behind Ma's death. Most of the evidence was circumstantial but they just knew it was her doing. They went into the kitchen and took the two samples of moonshine from the fridge, they lit the moonshine from the bowl containing the gingerbread doll, it burnt red, they lit the moonshine from the bottom of the bottle next to Ma's body, it burnt red. Willie went into Ma's chest in the bedroom and took out a bottle of her own moonshine, they took it into the kitchen and lit a small amount, it burnt bright blue.

There was no doubt now that she had drunk moonshine with lead in it. Willie knew they would find it in the autopsy but because it was bootleg would suspect that she had made a bad batch herself. Only he and Jane could find out the truth about what had happened.

As Willie was leaving the kitchen he noticed something on the kitchen floor, it was a gingerbread finger. It was the same size as his and Jane's but neither of them had lost a finger so that meant it had to be Fanny's. It looked as though she had trapped it in one of the cupboard doors and it had snapped off. Willie carefully picked it up with a piece of paper and put it into a plastic bag. When Sheriff Earl was back on duty he would ask him if it could be DNA tested it was no good asking Dwayne he was obviously brainless. Willie wanted to know why Fanny was so evil when she had come from the same dough as him and Jane.

Willie wrote everything down so they could conclude. Fanny had to be found before someone else suffered. He wrote about the dolls which were found in her locker at The El Tovar Hotel, about the gingerbread dolls Ma had found in the kitchen when Fanny had left and poor Tom the wood seller who was the victim of one of those dolls. He wrote down the results of his moonshine tests, there was no point hiding from Sheriff Earl about the moonshine, Ma was dead now and they would find it in her stomach anyway.

The next morning Sheriff Earl arrived, he told Jane and Willie how sorry he was that Ma Cahill was dead, he had contacted her son in Phoenix and he was making the necessary arrangements. Sheriff Earl told Willie that he would never get moonshine like the stuff Ma Cahill used to give him she was one of the best distillers of the stuff for miles around. She had supplied him and many others for years; it was a safe reliable moonshine. Willie couldn't believe what he was hearing; Ma was a bootleg moonshine supplier and had supplied the local police!

Sheriff Earl explained to Willie that moonshine would always be distilled and they couldn't stop it from happening completely, if they didn't have decent safe distillers they would end up with many deaths from red moonshine which had happened many years back. It was people like Ma Cahill who kept it safe. Almost everyone had some of Ma's in their home, hers always tasted the best but she wouldn't tell anyone why.

The other person who made a damn good moonshine was old Skippity Jack Moran, he and Ma swapped bottles of the stuff so they had some variety. It was actually Skippity Jack who had taught her to distil it and he still did most of it now as Ma had considerably slowed down her output due to her baking business

Sheriff Earl could see Willie was surprised but told him not to worry Ma Cahill's secret would go with her to the grave. Willie was glad Sheriff Earl was honest with him because he now felt he could trust him. He told Sheriff Earl that he believed Fanny was behind the death of Ma Cahill and showed him the list of evidence he had made, Sheriff Earl agreed that most of the evidence was circumstantial. Wille told him that he could not understand why Fanny could be so evil. He gave Sheriff Earl Fanny's finger and asked him if he could have it DNA tested because he wanted to know if she had something in her DNA which they didn't.

Sheriff Earl told Willie that it was very expensive to send something off for DNA testing and if he sent off a gingerbread finger he may well get fired from his job as well as be placed in a home for mentally deranged people. Willie looked disappointed; Sheriff Earl gave a sigh and took the finger from Willie he couldn't promise anything but he would see what he could do.

The next few days were very difficult; they contacted as many people as they could to tell them what had happened. Jane telephoned The El Tovar Hotel to see if Fanny had returned but she hadn't they had not seen her for days. Jane informed them about Ma Cahill and asked them to let her know if Fanny returned to the Hotel.

Sheriff Earl visited them and told them that they had found red moonshine in Ma Cahill's system, he was now very suspicious because he knew she would not have knowingly drank it, she must have thought it came from a trusted source.

He had been to question Skippity Jack Moran and removed some moonshine from his house for testing, his moonshine was good and Skippity Jack was devastated at the news that Ma was dead. A few days later with her son and grandson from Phoenix present, Willie, Jane, and all her friends and neighbours, Ma Cahill was laid to rest in the cemetery near her home. It was a very sad day and everyone cried. They all had their memories of her and no one had a bad word to say against her.

Two days after the funeral, Sheriff Earl telephoned to tell Jane and Willie that he had some news on the DNA sample, a friend of his in the forensic department had owed him a huge favour so he had called it in and asked him to test Fanny's finger.

The result was shocking, Fanny had the same DNA sequence as Jane and Willie, but she also had a foreign DNA in her system. The foreign DNA was tested and the results were put into a data base. They got a hit. The sinister thing was, Fanny was contaminated with the DNA of a wanted fugitive, and it was the same one who had called at Ma Cahill's house the night they had all come to life.

Sheriff Earl told them he suspected that Fanny had somehow come into contact with the wanted man and that is how his low profile DNA had entered her biscuit body, it was easily soaked in from his sweaty grubby hands, then they had been varnished and it was sealed in. Fanny was therefore part of this man and everything he represented as a person.

This was so creepy. What they needed to do was to find Fanny and the fugitive, individually they were dangerous but together they were lethal.

Sheriff Earl organised a search party for in and around the Canyon, he knew they would still be hiding there somewhere. Lots of people arrived at the house and they set it up as a base. There were search teams from all over, and also some to cover the Vegas side and the Utah side of the Canyon. Willie and Jane wanted to be part of the search; they wanted to see exactly where Fanny had been hiding and what she had been up to.

Sheriff Earl told them that they could be facing a lot of danger and if they went they would have to be partnered up with a search team officer who was armed. Willie thought this was a bit exciting and agreed, he was partnered up with an officer named Slick and Jane was partnered with an officer named Budd not their real names of course. They were each given a map and a radio, they were given full instructions that if they found the wanted pair they were to radio one of the bases immediately. There would be three bases, one at the house, one at Grand Canyon Village and one at Phantom Ranch.

The search was to start at dawn; they drove to Grand Canyon Village and camped for the night. Willie and Jane shared a tent with Slick and Budd. It was a bit of a strange night there were a lot of noises which were unfamiliar, Willie thought he had heard every sound associated with the Canyon, but there were some very odd ones outside the tent. One of the sounds was a roaring noise, it was very loud and distracting, it only happened for a few minutes, then it stopped. When the noise stopped he could hear the gruff voice of a man and a whimpering sound.

Willie looked around the tent. Everyone was asleep; he slowly unzipped the tent a tiny bit and looked outside. He could see a strange looking vehicle, it had two wheels and some sort of carriage on the side he had never seen anything like it before. Next to the vehicle a man was erecting a tent, he was huffing and puffing and muttering to himself, Willie then saw something move in the carriage, it was a small dog. It was the dog who was whimpering, he was also shivering he must have been cold. Willie watched what was going on; the man who was quite large and intimidating completed the tent and took some food and a flask out of a bag which was in the carriage. The dog looked up and the man said to him

"If you think your coming in the tent your wrong you smelly little bastard"

The dog was very upset, he cowered down with fear. Willie slowly unzipped the rest of the tent and stepped outside; he walked over to the dog and asked him if he was ok. The dog was very afraid but said that he was alright he was just cold and tired. Willie asked him what sort of vehicle he was travelling in and the dog told him it was a motorcycle with a side car. He told Willie that his name was Spike and he was travelling with his Master across America to see the sights. Willie was about to ask Spike why he was not allowed in the tent, when the most terrible stench arose from the side car making Willie gag. Spike apologised and said that he had a terrible flatulence problem and that was the reason he was not allowed in the tent.

Willie told Spike that he had a friend named Butt who also had a problem with severe flatulence so he was quite used to it, the only difference was Butts did not smell too bad where as Spike's was enough to make his eyes water and strip the varnish from his body. At that moment Spikes master opened his tent and walked over to the side car, he gave Spike some bread and water, Willie sat perfectly still in the shadows so the man wouldn't see him.

Unfortunately the man did see Willie because he took a flash light out of his pocket and switched it on making the shadows disappear and Willie completely visible.

"Well look here a giant gingerbread man looks like I have something to go with my coffee, smells pretty good too" said the man.

Willie was terrified he had never thought of himself as food until now. Everyone else saw him as a little person. The man picked Willie up and took him into the tent, Willie kept very still, and then he thought that if he did move the man may be freaked out and let him go. Just as he was about to say something and flap his arms about, Spike ran into the tent the man was cross with Spike and told him to go outside, Spike ran into the corner of the tent and sat down growling and refusing to move. He snarled, his teeth being revealed by his gums which were being pushed up over them, his eyes were wide open and he really looked the business.

"ok" said the man "Have it your way you sit in the tent and watch me eat this lovely yummy gingerbread man" He poured himself a coffee and sat down comfortably ready to eat Willie. As he opened his mouth to put Willie inside Spike let out a huge fart the like of which Willie had never heard even from Butt's arse, but the stench which even worse it was horrific. How the hell could something that small smell so bad. The man dropped Willie onto the floor and spilt his hot coffee all over himself, he jumped up in pain and ran out of the tent in search of cold water to save his man hood, as he did he tripped over the tent guide ropes and fell flat on his face.

Spike took Willie in his mouth and ran out of the tent with him, Willie was not a small gingerbread man but Spike was a small dog, he ran so fast Willie thought he was going to be dropped to the floor or sick the way he was being tossed around in Spike's mouth. Spike ran and ran Willie thought he would never stop. He shouted for Spike to slow down and told him he couldn't be away from the tents.

Spike was very frightened, Willie felt sorry for him he was concerned he would get badly punished if he went back to his owner. Spike slowed down a bit and eventually came to a stop he was panting and spat Willie out of his mouth.

Willie thought for a moment, he could take Spike with him down the Canyon. He was sure no one else would mind and Spike couldn't go back to his master now. He may even come in useful if his sense of smell was any good. Poor Spike, he did look very sorry for himself.

CHAPTER FIFTEEN

Willie and Spike couldn't go back to the tents because of Spike's owner, so they made their way back to the camp but stayed under the porch at The El Tovar Hotel. They didn't have the most comfortable night sleep but they were warm and safe. The next morning they were woken by the sound of Spike's owner starting up his bike, they looked out from their hiding place to see him leave. He had packed everything away so they knew he was not coming back, as he left he threw a bag over his shoulder containing Spikes belongings, not much just his passport, dog bowl and lead.

Willie was hungry and guessed that Spike would be too so they made their way to Willie's tent. Jane was making breakfast for Budd and Slick she had not even noticed Willie had not been in the tent and was surprised to see him walking towards her, she was even more surprised to see Spike but he immediately brought a smile to her face.

In the daylight Spike looked very funny, he was a small jack russle with wirery fur his face was very cute it was mostly white but had a black patch over his right eye, he had a bit of a hairy beard under his chin and a squint which was quite noticeable, it was as though he was straining to see something. His tummy was making the most horrendous noise he was very hungry. They sat down and Jane served breakfast. Slick and Budd joined them, they said that Spike would be a very useful addition to the search party and they welcomed him to join them. He looked very happy and wagged his tail.

They ate bacon and cowboy biscuits and drank lots of coffee, Spike thought it was wonderful because his owner had only ever fed him bread and water, as he sat and ate little tears of pleasure filled his eyes as he tasted flavours which he never knew existed.

While they were eating Budd explained to them what would be happening, he told them there was no need to be covert because it would look more suspicious, they should blend in like any other visitor to the Canyon. If either Jane or Willie were to see Fanny or the Fugitive, they should be calm note their locality and call it in. Willie told Spike he would explain everything to him on the way down the Canyon. They packed up their mules and set off towards the Bright Angel Trail.

Spike was squinting even more and Willie thought maybe the sun was affecting his eyes, he asked Spike if he was alright, maybe he would like to borrow a hat. Spike explained that he was light sensitive but also had an eye sight problem which he had specks for but in is escape from his master he had left them in the side car and they were not in the bag he threw. Willie took Spike into The El Tovar Hotel they would ask the receptionist if there was somewhere they could pick up some specs for him.

Emily was on reception and remembered Willie, he explained to her about Spike needing specs. There was nowhere in the Village where they could buy some but Emily pulled out a box from under the counter labelled "lost property" in the box there were lots of pairs, they had been left by guests and never claimed, some of them had been there for years so Emily told Spike to try them on to see if any of them were of any use to him. Willie helped him and soon they found a pair which were perfect, Spike was very happy he didn't even mind that they were obviously for a woman, he could see and that was all that mattered.

Despite looking hilarious Willie tried very hard not to laugh at Spike. He did look quite intelligent though with his specs on, when Jane saw him she thought he looked very cute. As they descended on the mules, Spike ran alongside he seemed to have settled in well with the group. He was amazed at how much he could see through his specs, he could see insects, flowers, birds and the colours of the Canyon walls it opened up a whole new world for him, these were so much better than his old specs.

Spike

It would take five and a half hours to reach Phantom Ranch which was to be their base inside the Canyon; they would eat, drink and rest there until the morning. Willie and Jane were looking forward to catching up with Ichee and Becci.

Although it was now September it was still hot during the day and they had to stop quite often to drink and tend to the mules,

Surprisingly the mules didn't mind Spike at all even though he was small and darted about a lot after dealing with Vicious Vicky not much bothered them. Willie explained to Spike the reason for their Canyon trip and told him that if he didn't want to go any further with them he could stay and wait for them at Phantom Ranch. Spike said that after having an owner like he had he was prepared for anything and was in on the search.

After a long trip they arrived at Phantom Ranch, they were very hot and tired, a camp had been made up especially for the search teams and a huge buffet of food was waiting for them. Everyone was assigned a tent and Jane being female had a cabin to herself. Once they had settled into their accommodation they sat on long wooden benches at long wooden tables with many other searchers, they could help themselves to whatever they wanted, but there was no alcohol allowed because they had to have clear heads, no one knew what Fanny and the Fugitive were capable of, they could be watching the camp as they all ate and slept.

While they were eating and drinking entertainment was provided for them, it was a guy who was excellent at playing the banjo, he was so good that no one could keep their feet still. One by one they got up to dance, this was good because they were acting as anyone else in the Canyon would act. The camp came alive, everyone was having a lovely time, and Jane thought that police really knew how to enjoy themselves even without alcohol. The dancing went on for a few hours until the police officer in charge said that it had to stop so they could all get to bed for a good sleep, they had an early start in the morning and needed to have their wits about them.

Willie settled into his tent with Spike, Budd and Slick, Jane was glad to have her own space as sharing with the guys the previous night had not been the best experience. As she settled down she was thinking about home and Ma Cahill, she was missing Baby who was being looked after by the Sheriff's wife Anna and she missed Floating Cloud who was with the Navajo.

It was very quiet during the night, the air was still and warm. As the camp slept the clouds rolled over the Canyon and a slight precipitation occurred it was so light no one knew and the ground was barely damp. Further away from the Canyon the rain had been a little heavier however and this was causing a potential danger. The dangers unknown to the campers were known to the authorities, at first light several helicopters entered the Canyon to warn people of the likelihood of a flash flood. When the search leader learnt of the dangers facing them, he addressed them all at breakfast time and explained the dangers of flash flooding and that they were at risk.

They were told they would have bulletins via their radios regularly to keep them up to date with any details of the flash flooding situation and they were in no circumstances to switch off their radios. Willie was worried he knew the devastation and death a flash flood could cause.

They were each given another map of the Canyon and each map was marked out with the search area for each group. Willie, Budd, Jane and Slick were to cover the Canyon and the contributory canyons between Grapevine rapid and Crystal rapid, this included Bright Angel Creek and Phantom Creek which had been the scene of a deadly flash flood fourteen years previously. They were nearer Phantom Ranch than any of the other groups because Jane and Willie were both targets of Fanny's and if that meant they could lure her to the Ranch it would be easier to apprehend her and the fugitive if he was with her.

Jane and Budd were to walk downstream from Phantom Ranch and Willie, Slick and Spike were to make their way to Phantom Creek via Bright Angel Creek, they needed to check Fanny was not hiding near the Ranch; there would be no point in searching further if she was near them. With their back packs on and their police issue boots and radios, they commenced with the search. Jane gave Willie a hug as they parted and told him to take care. She was one hell of a girl, gutsy and intelligent, but Willie would still worry about her even though he knew she was in good hands with Budd.

Slick was a good guy he was very large and looked very powerful, he told Willie that he enjoyed the search team very much and had a nose for things. Willie asked him if he had been to the Canyon previously, Slick said he had been many times because he loved the Canyon so much, this pleased Willie it was nice to be in the company of someone who enjoyed the Canyon as he did.

Slick told him about a place called Montezuma Castle which was in Arizona, a dwelling which had been built in the side of a limestone cliff between Flagstaff and Phoenix; it was twenty rooms high and had a history going back over one thousand years. It was a beautiful place where people had lived very basic lives for many years near the gentle flowing of Beaver Creek. Slick told Willie that it was a very peaceful place and it seemed to emanate a great sense of calmness and tranquillity, his mother had visited there once and was very stressed because she had some complications in her life but as soon as she arrived at Montezuma, she had an overwhelming feeling of calm and well being, something which she could not explain but found most reassuring.

Willie thought that he would like to visit Montezuma Castle and would definitely put it on his list of things to do. He thought it was very nice that Slick was in tune with nature and his surroundings it was not often you found someone as tough looking as Slick with a soft side to him, Willie was in good company. Chatting to Slick also made the time go quicker, they looked for any signs of Fanny and the Fugitive along the way but they found nothing so far.

With so many people using the Canyon Slick was concerned it would be difficult to associate anything they found with Fanny but Willie knew that he would know evidence related to her when he saw it, and he knew Jane would also. Fanny was unique in many ways she left clues which she knew were circumstantial and could not be proven to be linked to her, but Willie and Jane knew differently.

While they were walking and getting to know each other better Slick stopped in his tracks, he could hear something, it sounded like thunder, he knew immediately what it was at that very second, his

125

radio blasted out a warning of a flash flood, it was heading down Bright Angel Creek. Slick told Willie to get as high as he could, they had just entered Bright Angel Creek and frantically looked around for somewhere higher.

Slick told Willie to climb, the walls were a seventy degree angle and they could make it higher if they were quick. Willie looked up stream and saw it, a huge six feet wall of water which was red in colour and was carrying all sorts of debris with it; he grabbed Spike and forced him into Slick's back pack, they climbed as fast as they could to get out of the way of this horrific surge of water, Slick made it to about 8ft and hauled Willie up behind him. They both clung to the side walls as the water caught up with them, two feet below them was the deadly torrent it consumed everything in its way and carried it down towards the Phantom Creek confluence.

The noise was horrendous and the water splashed and bumped the walls as though it were trying to escape from something. Boulders were being swept along as though they were footballs, trees and bushes had been up rooted and were being unwillingly taken without any effort at all. It was unbelievable; the power behind this wall of water was extremely frightening but awesome to watch. Willie and Slick clung on to the Canyon wall as the water seemed to shake the foundations of the stone. This was nature at one of its most angry moments but it was also a privilege to watch.

It took a long time for the water to pass and calm to be restored. The area was wet and muddy. They had no idea if another wall of water was on the way. Slick radioed in as soon as the water and the noise went and told base camp what had happened, they advised them that helicopters had been to the area and there was no immediate danger of another water wall. Willie, Slick and Spike were relieved and they continued further up Bright Angel Creek.

Spike had by now wiggled his way out of the back pack and was running alongside Willie; he was having a good sniff of the freshly relocated silt. As he sniffed around, he saw something sticking out of the mud, it smelt very familiar, although it was dirty and a little soggy, he knew the smell, he barked to get Willie's attention as he and Slick had walked on a little. Slick went back to see what Spike had found. He examined it but could not see what all the fuss was about; it was just the soggy remains of a biscuit. Willie took a look to see what Spike had found and was horrified. It was the remains of a gingerbread doll and there was only one person this could have come from, Fanny!

Willie explained to Slick the significance of the doll, it was very possible it had just been swept away from where Fanny was hiding, which meant she must be somewhere along the route the water had taken, but it was also possible that she purposely threw the doll into the water to cause harm to its subject. Willie carefully removed the remains of the doll from the mud, it was a hot day and they needed to remove it before the sun dried the mud and compacted the doll into it. Willie placed it on a rock to dry and be examined.

There were no distinguishing features to connect it with anyone he or Fanny would know. Slick suggested they had a coffee and something to eat and wait for the doll to dry in the sun for a while he would then place it in an evidence bag. Spike had been a very useful dog he had found a possible piece of evidence and should be very proud of himself; Slick gave Spike a reward of a slice of beef jerky and a packet of roasted peanuts.

As Willie and Slick drank their coffee, a call came over the radio informing all searchers that the risk of flash flooding was now at a minimal, however many boulders had been dislodged creating a risk of them becoming unstable and falling. They would have to be very careful.

Spike seemed to be rather unsettled and was sniffing everything, he could not keep still. Willie thought it was because he could see so much through his new specs but it wasn't. Spike could sense danger from somewhere and it was not far away he couldn't wait to get searching again he felt sure they would find something soon.

Soon the doll was dry and they were able to move on, Spike led the way and Slick let him, he could see he was on to something. It was amazing the way Spike took hold of a scent and followed it. His nose was down to the ground and his tail was wagging he had no idea what was coming over him; he just had an overwhelming urge to do doggy things.

As he sniffed his specs moved up and down on his nose and he did look funny. As he moved along in search mode Spike tasted things, things were not really edible but he just had to taste them, he had never been taught to use his taste buds independently as he had been stolen by his Master when he was a tiny pup out of his basket, he had not even been old enough to leave his mother, the horrible man had stopped off to buy eggs and milk from the farm where Spike had been born, reached inside the basket and snatched poor Spike from the comfort of his mother.

As he sniffed and tasted his way along, Spike licked up some sort of insect from the ground, it tasted disgusting and he yelped, he turned around to Willie and Slick and the taste made his lips curl up over his teeth and he hissed sticking his tongue out between his teeth. He went to the Canyon wall and licked it furiously trying to remove the taste from his mouth. Slick collapsed with laughter he had not seen anything so funny in all his life. Willie was laughing too and then he realised something, Spike was a mini Butt, with the way he hissed and curled his gums over his teeth, how uncanny to find two good friends with the same habit.

CHAPTER SIXTEEN

While Willie, Slick and Spike were exploring Bright Angel Creek for clues, Jane and Budd were heading towards Grapevine Rapid. They were to cover every part of the river on the north side of the Colorado on the way up to the rapid and cover each part on the south side on the way back down stream to Phantom Ranch. They had been very lucky when the flood hit, they had been opposite Phantom Creek and because of the radio message had been able to move to safer ground, they were shocked at the speed and velocity of the wall of water and thought that anyone in its way would not have stood a chance.

Budd was a very good searcher; he had not been down the Canyon before so Jane's limited knowledge was better than his. He found the environment both awe inspiring, but rather daunting, the thought of being a mile deep into the earth freaked him out a bit. Jane was a good help to him because she told him about her experiences of the Canyon when she had been on the raft with Willie, he was very interested in her experience and it did help him to feel a little more settled. He had been to many places while he was a search officer and had a lot of interesting tales to tell.

Again, as with Willie and Slick, getting to know each other and sharing stories helped to pass the time. Jane explained to Budd about Fanny, the way she behaved and the gingerbread dolls. This information was very important because the gingerbread doll theory Jane and Willie had come up with had not been taken entirely seriously by the search team leaders, but Budd said he took any information seriously as the most bizarre of things can happen.

While the search team searched and other visitors to the Canyon went about their day, deep within a slot canyon in a side canyon Fanny was hiding confident that she would not be found. She had a natural ability to be covert but also a brilliantly agile way of moving within the Canyon as though she were part of it, she could have easily been a breeze or a grain of sand being blown about she was that inconspicuous.

The clues she left were not accidental and were her way of teasing and tormenting those in pursuit of her. She was of course not hiding alone; in the slot canyon with her was the fugitive who had told her his name was Alvin Buster Hung. He was a truly evil piece of work with eyes which would make you want to kneel down and pray for protection from the devil when you saw them it was hard to believe he was only twenty years old.

Al B Hung and Fanny were two of a kind and while they sat personalising gingerbread dolls they sniggered and laughed at the thought of the huge search party which was looking for them. Yes they knew all about the search party, and they had copies of the maps and search areas, they had both visited Phantom Ranch the previous night and acquired information about the search. Fanny had actually been in Jane's cabin and chillingly stood over her while she was sleeping. They knew they would be up against some of the best searchers in the country but that just made their days much more exciting the challenge was so tempting and full of fun.

Both fanny and Al decided they were going to have as much fun with the search party as they could. Fanny looked at Al and wondered why he was so incredibly evil and sly, she was fascinated with him. When Willie had taken her to Separation Canyon, Fanny had been helping Al. She had been giving him food and water so he could be safely tucked away from anyone, they had then moved from Separation Canyon to their present location because they wanted to cause as much trouble as possible and Phantom Ranch was a good place for them to do it.

Alvin had been born in Tombstone Arizona and was a bad egg from day one. His mother had been very sweet and loving but had been married off to a man who was a close relative of hers, this resulted in Alvin being totally abnormal. Although his mother Daisy was caring and tried very hard to bring Al up in the correct way, it seemed the forces were against her. His father was a mean man who blamed Daisy for everything; he liked his drink and would hit Daisy about on a daily basis when he had a skinful of alcohol. Most sons would have stood up for their mother in a situation like this but not Al, he had no respect for his mother and treated her as though she were put on this earth to serve him and him alone, an attitude he had no doubt inherited from his father.

The more Al and his Father Buck treated Daisy badly the more she shrank into a shell. She became very controlled and was not even allowed out of the house unless it was to get food or do something for either of the men in her life.

One day while Daisy was cleaning the house, a man knocked at the door, he was a stranger and had been travelling for days on his horse. He and his horse were in need of food and water and Daisy who was in the house alone nervously offered him what he needed. When the man was refreshed, he thanked her and asked her why she was so nervous he said he would not hurt her and she had been very kind to him.

Daisy had never told a soul about her life with Buck and Al but for some strange reason she felt compelled to tell the stranger about her measly existence. The man told her that his name was Matthew and he didn't understand why such a lovely kind lady as her should be treated in such a way, he said that he adored his mother and so did his father, every woman should be treated with respect and kindness as she was the most important part of the home and family.

This was very strange to Daisy, she didn't consider herself as important even her own father had been very hard towards her. Matthew told her to get whatever she needed together and he would take her with him, she didn't have to stay here she should be enjoying her life. Daisy said there was no way she could leave her husband and son, but when she thought about the reasons for staying she realised it was because she was frightened of them finding her, not because she loved them.

She suddenly found a surge of courage and a sense of adventure, without giving it another thought she grabbed a bag and stuffed as many of her of her personal belongings into it as she could.

Without leaving a single clue as to where she was going or who she was with Daisy took hold of Matthew's hand and he helped her up onto the back of his horse. Making sure they were not seen by anyone they worked their way around the back of the town then off into the safety and vastness of the surrounding desert.

When her husband and son arrived home from the local saloon they found an empty house, no coffee pot on the stove and no food prepared. After smashing up most of the house in search of Daisy they both sat and drank themselves into unconsciousness on the floor. This was good for Matthew and Daisy as it gave them a good head start on their escape. The next morning the two abandoned men vowed that they would search for Daisy and never give up until they found her. No one had seen her leave so they had no clues to follow.

Daisy and Matthew rode to Texas where his parents lived and he looked after her providing her with a place to live and a job to support her. She became part of Matthew's family and was treated like a daughter by his parents Alison and Mark. At the age of thirty five she could start to live her life, she had been married at fourteen years of age and gave birth to Al when she was fifteen.

While Daisy was at last living a life she deserved to live, Al and Buck never stopped looking for her, as far as Buck was concerned she had made a fool of him and the town folk would think him weak for not being able to keep his woman. What Buck didn't realise however was the town folk adored Daisy and were very concerned over her disappearance and thought Buck had murdered her and hidden her body, because of this Al and Buck un known to them were being hunted by the authorities.

The longer they looked for Daisy the more bitter and twisted they became both increasing each other's anger by aggravating each other about it. One day while in a saloon bar in a small town, they were approached by a man who asked them if they wanted to run some cattle for a couple of days because his men had let him down, they would be paid for their trouble and fed and watered along the way, the cattle needed to be taken from Arizona to Mexico. With nothing else better to do they agreed to do the cattle run, they may even come across Daisy on the way.

The man who hired them said his name was Hickory Smoke stupidly the two of them believed him, he said they should wear cowboy hats and neckerchiefs at all times to prevent being bitten by insects attracted by the cattle, he also gave them both a gun in case they needed to kill predators who may want to relieve them of some of the stock.

Buck and Al took the money and guns and covered up their heads and faces with the hats and neckerchiefs Hickory gave them. They were also provided with a horse each and told that when they got as far as the Mexican border there would be someone there to meet them and swap their horses for fresh ones.

Of course this was not all as it seemed, Hickory Smoke was a cattle rustler from nowhere in particular and was wanted in four states, he knew he was being caught up with and had to get rid of the herd of cattle he currently had because he needed to keep a low profile. The guns he had given to Al and Buck had been used to kill the man whose cattle he had stolen and injure the sheriff who had tried to detain him. Al and Buck had no idea of the trouble they had been passed on.

They took the cattle on and drove them north east towards the border, there were two hundred cattle in total and every now and then they had to stop and count them to make sure they were all present. This took time and unknown to them the authorities were tracking the cattle which were branded with the owners mark.

The first three days went well they drove the cattle and seemed to settle into the routine. They started off at first light and stopped when the sun went down. On the fourth night they were near the border so decided to stop and set up camp for the night a little earlier.

They would be getting fresh horses in the morning and could hopefully move on a little faster. During the early hours of the morning, Al was woken by something cold on his temple, it was still quite dark and he couldn't see what it was, he sat up, his hands were immediately cuffed to the rear. He called to his father but he was already in custody also handcuffed.

They were both taken to a local town and put into jail, the next day there were to appear in the local court charged with cattle rustling, murder, and attempted murder, they were not guilty of any of these crimes but all the evidence stacked against them.

The court found them guilty and they were to be transported to the state prison just outside Phoenix. While being loaded onto the prison transport vehicle, Al became sick and had to be taken to a local hospital; his father was transported without him and began to serve his life sentence.

Al was diagnosed with appendicitis and operated on; he had to stay in the hospital for a number of weeks because he developed an infection. During that time he befriended a young nurse named Mary who he charmed, she for some strange reason fell in love with him and was under his spell. He was young and not bad looking when he dropped the evil glint.

Realising this could be used to his advantage, Al told the poor girl a load of lies about loving her and wished he had never done what he had done because he could have married her and they could have spent the rest of their lives together. He also told her he had a lot of money stashed away in a secret place at his home in Tombstone and if he could get to it they could run away together and live a very privileged life. Mary felt very sorry for him and because she loved him so much she agreed to help him escape. Al was under twenty four hour guard at the hospital so it was not going to be easy.

Mary took a large laundry basked into Al's room filled with sheets, the guard on duty in his room started talking to her and flirting so she flirted back, she asked him if he would like a cup of coffee. When she went to make the coffee, she crushed up a handful of sleeping tablets and stirred them into his drink. She gave the guard his coffee and went off to do some of her chores. She returned half an hour later to see he was out cold in his chair. She took the guards keys and unchained Al, he climbed into the laundry basket covered himself with the sheets and Mary pushed it out of the hospital no one suspected a thing. They caught a train from the local station and headed towards Flagstaff.

While they were on the train Mary asked him why they were not heading to Tombstone to get the money he had stashed away. Al had never been questioned by a woman in his life and was not about to let it start, he told her he was doing things his way and she was to shut up and go along with it. At that very moment Mary looked into his eyes and saw for the first time pure evil looking back at her, she got up from her seat and walked towards the door of the train compartment she felt a strong urge to get away from this man. Whatever it was she loved about him was yanked out of her and all she was left with was the terrifying feeling of needing to get away from him as quickly as she could.

As Mary opened the door she was pulled back by Al, she struggled with him and put up a fight, he was stronger than her but she was a good match for him. Eventually realising he was going to have to stop her from struggling before she brought attention to them, he hit her head hard against the window not once but several times, he hit her head so hard he cracked the glass in the window. With blood streaming down her face and barely conscious Mary still put up a fight, she desperately tried to scream out but Al had his hands tight around her neck.

He pulled her to the floor and momentarily took his hands from her throat to hold her hands still as she was clawing at him scratching his skin. As he did this she kicked him in his private area, although in immense pain and winded, Al still didn't let her go, he grabbed at his sleeve and pulled it off stuffing it into her mouth to stop her from screaming, he took his belt off and put it around her neck pulling it tight until she took her last breath.

The injuries Mary sustained were horrific, severe head trauma and strangulation, the only thing she did wrong was fall in love. Al opened the window of the train and pushed Mary's body through it, then he climbed through the window himself and jumped from the train, he knew the police would be waiting for him at the station in Flagstaff

Al made his way towards the Canyon; he knew he had more chance of hiding there and not being found. It was a long way to the Canyon and he couldn't use any form of transport, even if he stole a car it would be reported stolen and he would bring attention to himself. For the next couple of days Al walked towards the Canyon looking for food and shelter where ever he could, water was the main problem, he couldn't find enough to keep him hydrated and it was very hot.

Al decided it may be an idea to take shelter during the day and walk during the night when it was cooler. He found an old shack in a wooded area and opened the door; it was cool and dark inside so he settled down and rested.

He had a thought, if there was a shack in the middle of nowhere there must have been water available, there was evidence that someone had lived there or at least spend a lot of time there, he went outside and had a look. He could hear the very faint sound of water and as he looked around he saw a small brook running through the trees. He went back to the shack and looked for something to collect water in, he found a plastic bottle and a metal mug, and he filled the bottle and the mug.

He decided to spend the rest of the day at the shack, he found some cans of food which he opened by hitting them against a rock, they contained corned beef and vegetables. His pathetic existence haunted the shack until nightfall when he decided to continue on his way to the Canyon. Although it was very dark, the moon did lend some light to the earth so he could just about see when he put one foot in front of the other.

He knew his bottle of water would not last long so constantly looked out for another source. He arrived at the Navajo Reservation, the women were asleep but some of the men were around the fire, he sneaked up behind them and stole some meat and biscuits, they knew he was there but ignored him; he also helped himself to water filling his bottle to the rim.

Moving on he walked as far as he could before the temperature became too hot for him to continue, he took shade under an overhanging rock. When the evening drew in bringing slightly cooler air, he continued to walk. Eventually he came to a small house he could smell something wonderful, freshly baked biscuits. He moved closer to the house and on the porch he could see three giant gingerbread biscuits, they were amazing they must have each been two feet tall. He moved closer towards them the smell was hypnotising, he reached out and grabbed one his sweaty fingers gripping around it. He directed the biscuit towards his mouth.

"Put my Fanny down"

A woman in her early forties was standing behind him and she meant business she was very angry and had a shot gun in her hand. He felt the urge to hit her hard to the ground, he could then take what he wanted, but if someone found her they would know it was him and where he was heading besides he didn't know how good she was with that gun.

She told him that if he sat still and didn't touch her gingerbreads she wouldn't put a bullet in his arse. She was pointing the gun at his head but said she knew one end of his body to the other but reckoned he had dough for brains. She said she would go into the house and get him some food if he didn't move.

He promised to do as she said, and she went inside returning a few minutes later with food and a thermos of coffee. She gave it to him and he went on his way.

For weeks he wandered the Canyon, he survived by stealing food and water from people but was always careful not to be seen. One day he sneaked up to The El Tovar Hotel, he really wanted a beer and thought he could steal a few from there. He smelt the wonderful smell of biscuits being baked and sneaked into the kitchen to take some. He saw Fanny and she saw him, he recognised her from Ma Cahill's house and they immediately knew they had a strong connection, from that day they became close, she had part of his DNA, and that was enough for them both to start an evil tirade which had no reason behind it but pure hatred for others.

She provided food and water for him while he hid in the depths of the Canyon, She would sneak onto helicopters and go into the Canyon and back again, that was how she was able to get between there and the hotel so quickly.

They had a wonderful time together plotting evil and enrolling others do join them, Vicious Vicky did not need much persuading and they were also joined by an evil army of squirrels who spied on their subjects for them reporting any information back to them that was how Fanny always knew where Willie and Jane were.

CHAPTER SEVENTEEN

The Canyon was buzzing, the flash flood danger alert had been lowered and people were starting to venture out again although being very cautious. Many had witnessed the surge as it entered the Colorado and had been shocked at the power it had. Jane and Budd searched everywhere for clues, but found nothing.

Slick and Willie however were on to something; Spike had picked up a scent and was going crazy. He ran around in circles, Willie asked him what was wrong and he told him he could smell the scent of an extremely unwashed human and blood.

Slick looked around and hanging on a rock he found a piece of rag, it contained diluted, smudged blood and looked as though someone had washed it off themselves. He placed it into an evidence bag, he needed someone to collect this as soon as possible so he could get it off to a lab for DNA testing, as it may belong to the fugitive. He radioed to ask if someone could collect the evidence, he did not want to leave the trail they were on and if the blood did belong to the fugitive he did not want the helicopters hovering and flushing him out of his hiding place in the wrong direction.

An officer met them and took both the blood sample and the gingerbread doll sample; he was told by Budd that the gingerbread sample had to go to Sheriff Earl as he would know all about it and what he had to do. The officer than made his way back to Phantom Ranch where he arranged to have the samples flown to the rim.

In the slot canyon Fanny and Al were busy making plans and were joined by the squirrels. Among the squirrels however was one who didn't like Fanny or Al, she was a good little squirrel who had watched Willie, Jane and Ichee when they had been at Phantom Ranch the time Ichee had had his mouth washed out with soap by Jane. She had seen how nice they were and how much Willie adored and respected the Canyon, she too adored it and unlike the other squirrels did not take her environment for granted and she hated anything or anyone who brought badness into her beautiful world. The squirrel was called Catherine she had been named after St Catherine and was gentle and kind.

She went along with the other squirrels who were all male to gather as much information as she could, she was very clever and had a secret urge to be a government agent, she used to love acting out spy scenes. Now she found herself spying for real and was excellent at it.

She asked the other squirrels open questions pretending that because she was a girl she was slow to take on what they were all doing, the intelligence she gathered was amazing. As soon as she got the opportunity she would introduce herself to Willie or Jane who ever she came across first and tell them what she knew.

She decided to go on a recognisance mission to see if anyone was getting near to the hide out, none of the other squirrels were suspicious, she told them she was going to do some exploring they were glad to be rid of her and her questions so off she went. Other female squirrels were looking after their home and babies but not Catherine she was destined for other things.

She left the slot canyon and headed south towards Bright Angel Creek. She kept to higher ground so she could see but not be seen; she scurried along on a mission. Around her waist she wore a cat collar and on the collar hung several items any spy should have. She had a note book, a digital camera, a compass, a knife and a small bag containing other various items, she always seemed to have something in the bag for every eventuality.

Suddenly she stopped, her small ears had picked something up, she could hear Spike whimpering and barking. Covertly running from rock to rock, and ducking behind shrubs and boulders Catherine soon approached Willie, Slick and Spike, she sat on her bottom and slid down the seventy degree Canyon wall at an impressive speed landing right in front of the whimpering Spike.

Spike was so freaked out by her immediate and surprise appearance that he jumped about six feet in the air, and let out a massive fart. Slick turned around to see what the noise was, he thought the fart was a loose boulder heading towards them but then the stench of the fart hit him and he realised as he gagged that Spike had dropped his guts.

"Oh you sick dog go and take a shit will you" he said, Spike looked at him, he was sure that if taking a shit to get rid of his farts was the answer it would have occurred to him to do it a long time ago. As though Slick could tell what Spike was thinking, he shook his head at his own stupidity at pointing out the obvious. Lucky for Catherine she was not downwind of Spikes recent flatulence addition so was not affected by the smell.

She stood on a small rock in front of them to get their attention. Slick was immediately interested because of the utility belt around her waist, but to him, a mere human all she was letting out was a series of continual squeaks, Spike and Willie could understand what she was saying though and translated it to Slick.

Catherine told them about the place where Al and Fanny were hiding, she told them about the army of squirrels who were spying on them and about the dolls which they had lined up along the slot canyon walls. She explained to them that she had seen Jane and Willie before and had witnessed how nice they were and wanted to be on their side.

Obviously she did make them suspicious, why would she go against squirrel kind and be the only one who wanted to go against Fanny and the fugitive. Could she be trusted?

Slick knew the real name of the fugitive and wondered if she would confirm it; this may prove that she was on the right path to telling the truth. She obviously knew she would be doubted and told

Willie that she would tell them anything they wanted her to as long as she knew the answer.

She confirmed the fugitive was Alwyn Buster Hung and that he was twenty years old, he came from Tombstone Arizona and had been on the run from the authorities for four weeks since he escaped from a hospital. She confirmed that Fanny was contaminated by his DNA and they were both working together on a master plan to cause an event which would hurt a lot of people.

Willie asked her if the evil deed they had planned was to do with the gingerbread dolls they had been creating, Catherine said that was one of the plans but the other one was worse and much more imminent. Slick suggested they sat down and had a coffee; Catherine could then tell them exactly what she knew he could write it down and call it in.

Willie said he would make the coffee and lit a small fire to heat some fresh water, he also had some ingredients to knock up a few cowboy biscuits, the smell and the presence of the fire was not a problem they were only doing what any other Canyon explorer would be doing. They sat down and Catherine told them that Al and Fanny were fascinated by the amount of people who had thrown themselves off the rim or had fallen because they had been stupid enough not to take notice of safety advice.

They wanted to make as many gingerbread people as they could and give them to visitors at the most popular view points, made by evil hands these dolls would not need to be turned into an individual by adding personal snippings of hair, skin etc. When people had these dolls they would be compelled to walk to the edge of the Canyon and then fete would take over. They also planned to give them out at the sky walk.

Slick was horrified, they had to be caught before they did this, how the hell did Fanny have the means to bake these dolls inside a slot canyon?

Catherine told them that Fanny had created a small oven at the top end of the slot canyon where they were hiding, she had a small metal bin with a lid and had partly buried it in the sand to keep it hot, as the day became hotter the heat inside the can turned it into an oven, she was able to cook two gingerbread dolls in there at a time, they took twenty minutes to cook and she had eight hours of direct sunlight at the correct temperature to bake them, she was producing six dolls per hour which was forty eight dolls per day and she had been baking them for ten days now so she had at least four hundred and eighty gingerbread dolls.

This was a serious problem, they needed to be stopped and the dolls destroyed. Worst of all they still had dolls in the slot canyon which were personalised and could be used remotely to punish those who were linked to them. Catherine said she realised it was difficult for them to believe her but they had to believe and trust in someone if she led them to the slot canyon they could see for themselves what they were up to.

Willie did trust Catherine, she knew about the dolls the same as he and Jane did, Slick was becoming more convinced by her and Willie had made him aware of the dolls earlier that day. Willie made a second pot of coffee. They sat down and had a good think, Slick knew that planning this was the key to a successful capture, they would not call it in just yet because they needed to be sure Catherine's information was genuine and it would be wrong to pull other search officers in from other parts of the Canyon until they knew they were on the right track.

After a coffee overload they all needed a pee, Spike took Slicks advice and told Willie he would try and have a poo. Slick told Willie to tell him if he did it anywhere near where they were sitting he would be in big trouble. Willie went for a pee behind a rock, while he was writing his name with it on the rock in full concentration, something wet and warm touched his back, he jumped and turned around, it was Butt!

"Told ya I would smell your coffee and biscuits" he said. Willie was thrilled to see him and had tears running down his face he hugged Butt tightly around his neck, Butt discretely used his tail to brush off the pee which had splashed on him when Willie had turned around quickly. The pals were once again reunited. Butt was rather puzzled that Willie had returned to the Canyon so soon after the first trip, Willie briefly explained to him about the search for Fanny, the death of Ma Cahill and the information they had received from Catherine the squirrel. Butt actually knew Catherine and was able to confirm that she was one of the nicest squirrels he had ever met and he did not generally trust squirrels.

They walked back to the coffee pot and biscuits, Butt helped himself much to the amazement of Slick. Willie introduced Butt to Slick, he knew Catherine so there was no need for introductions they just hugged. Butt looked at his coffee mug with the look Willie knew, he told Butt he didn't have any, they were trying to be careful what they said in front of Slick,

Catherine reached into her handy pouch and produced a shot of moonshine for Butt, Slick at this point let it go over his head, a squirrel who thought she was a spy, a walking talking gingerbread man, a dog with an arse like a sewer and now a mule with an addiction to illegal substances, what was the point in showing any objection, he was obviously the odd one out, the weird one.

Butt actually liked Slick, he could sense his connection with nature and the Canyon he pushed his Star Butts coffee in his direction to see if he was a cool dude, Slick picked up the coffee mug and tried it, he smiled and then finished it off much to Butts delight but slight annoyance, he had only been offering a taste.

Willie told Slick that Butt was thrilled he liked his coffee and told him it was called a Star Butts and the reason behind the name. Slick thought the reasoning behind the name was a bit miss leading until he stood up and sat firmly back down again. Pulling himself together he stood up again and moved forward, they all knew it had an effect on him but out of politeness pretended not to notice and thought it would be rude to mention it.

Spike was back; he had respected the feelings of the group and taken himself off quite a way to do his doggy deed. He had also done the responsible thing and buried it because to be honest the smell was so bad even he felt like vomiting. It was rather a surprise to see a friendly mule with the group though, Willie introduced them and Butt thought Spike was brilliant, he had a funny face, was small and cute, and looked full of fun and personality. Spike was not sure about Butt, he liked him but was a bit jealous, he now had a rival for Willie's affections and they had known each other for longer than he and Willie had.

Slick asked Catherine how far away they were from Fanny and Al; she said it would take about an hour to get there. Slick said they should not walk any further until they had devised a plan, he had an idea he wanted to share with them. If Catherine could go to the slot canyon where they were hiding and remove one of the gingerbread dolls they may be able to get someone to make some exactly the same so they could somehow switch them with Fanny's, they would have to make more than what she currently had to allow for breakages and the fact that her collection was increasing every day and she probably accounted for each one, but he was sure it could be done.

As soon as they were ready to swap the dolls Catherine could go and count them so they knew exactly how many to swap and at the same time someone else could accidently stamp on her oven to stop her making any more. Then they could get the search officers to cover each of the view points and let Fanny and Al do their deed, that way they would be caught in the act, Fanny's dolls would be kept as evidence and they would hopefully prevent any further gingerbread induced accidents.

Willie thought it was an excellent idea, if he could contact Jane, maybe she could go to The El Tovar Hotel and ask someone to help her make the gingerbread dolls using their kitchen, he was sure Mr Jones would agree to help as he knew Fanny.

Catherine scooped up some of the thick silt from the side of the creek she would use it to make an indentation of Fanny's gingerbread doll cutter so they knew the shape and size would be the same. The only problem was taking one of the dolls Fanny knew how many she had. Catherine decided the best thing would be to take a picture and a small sample of one so that the minimum disruption was made. She headed off towards the hideout while slick and the others planned the rest.

When she arrived at the slot canyon it was very busy, the production of the dolls was in full swing and Fanny had added another three ovens. Fanny had now enlisted the help of a few squirrels to help take the dolls into the slot canyon stack and store them. Al was sleeping off some beers he had stolen from some hikers a few days previously. Catherine thought helping with the dolls would give her a good opportunity to gather the evidence; she blended in with the helpers. She worked on the stacking and storing, when no one was looking she took out her camera and took a photo of one of the dolls, she also took out her measure and held it against the doll to photograph the dimensions. Lastly she went to the centre of the pile of dolls and snapped the leg off one of them and shoved it into her pouch.

The next bit would be tricky, she had to get hold of the cutter to copy the shape, it would take seconds but Fanny was using it constantly when she did momentarily put it down it was too put the dolls in the ovens and she was never far from it. Catherine sat and thought, she was at that moment sitting above Fanny on a rock, she took her water bottle from around her neck and poured some of the water into her paws she positioned herself over Fanny and shook the water so it fell like rain drops onto Fanny and her ovens.

Fanny immediately shoved the dolls she had just cut into the ovens and closed the lids, she ran into the slot canyon to take shelter and to find something to cover the ovens with in case the rain cooled them down. As she ran off Catherine ab sailed down the rock with amazing speed and precision, made a copy of the cutter and was gone within a flash. As fast as she could she made her way back to Willie, Slick, Butt and Spike.

Catherine took out her camera and showed the pictures to Willie and Slick, then she took out the gingerbread foot and explained to Willie that it was so they could get the mixture as close to Fanny's as possible and lastly gave them the muddy silt with the cutter shape on it which by now had dried in the sun and become nice and hard.

Slick told them all they were not to go any further, they were to go back to Phantom Ranch and report what they knew. They could get Catherine's photos printed off get someone to make a cutter from the shape she had provided and get to work on the gingerbread dolls.

After three hours they reached Phantom Ranch, when Slick had told the officer in charge what they knew, he got onto his radio and called off the search, he agreed with Slick's plan and said an operation would be set up and it was important that Fanny and Al were left alone to cook their plan.

Slowly search teams returned and settled back into the camp they were all de briefed for any possible clues but there were none from anyone else, they were told to rest, eat and then they would be briefed on the developments and the operation which was going to be set up. Because Willie, Slick and their team knew more than anyone about the situation they were assigned tasks.

Willie was to ask Jane to make the gingerbread dolls. Slick was to organise who would go where, Spike and Butt were told to stay at Phantom Ranch and look for any signs of squirrels who looked suspicious and Catherine was to brief the team on the layout of the hideaway and the access to it.

At Grand Canyon Village a black smith was commissioned to make a copy of the cutter, he made fifty of them in total and his wife gathered an army of local women from the women's institute to help with the dolls, none of them were told what they were for due to security risks, they were just told to go to the hotel the next day to mix and cut gingerbread dolls, they were not to breath a word to anyone about what they were doing. Barbara the blacksmiths wife ran the local women's institute and gave her word that the women would keep quiet; even she just got on with the job and asked no questions.

At 5am the next morning Barbara marched her army of women to the kitchen at The El Tovar Hotel; Mr Jones supplied breakfast and coffee for the women and plied them with food and drinks throughout the day. They worked tirelessly mixing, cutting and baking. By 6 pm that evening the women had made four thousand gingerbread dolls. They also stored several batches of dough in the fridge ready to make more at short notice if they needed to.

The dolls were carefully stacked and placed into large plastic containers ready to be transported down the Canyon. Within two hours every gingerbread doll which had been made was at Phantom Ranch after being taken down by helicopter.

The only problem they now had was how they were going to get the opportunity to swap them over. Slick gathered Willie, Butt, Catherine and Spike together and they headed back to Bright Angel Creek.

CHAPTER EIGHTEEN

On the way back to Bright Angel Creek to carry out "Operation Baking Soda"

Slick who had not earned that name for nothing, explained to each of them what he wanted them to do. They all had a very important role to play and the timing was crucial. Each of them was very nervous because they didn't want to let anyone down and be the one to expose the operation.

The gingerbread doll which Spike had found in the slurry was analysed and it was found to have the same ingredients as the foot cut off one of the ones in the hide out by Catherine, it must have been a reject or possibly caught up in the flash flood and carried downstream. It also had a DNA sequence the same as Fanny's finger which meant it was one of the dolls intended to cause death to someone.

A convey of twenty mules was brought in to help transport the safe gingerbread dolls to the hideout. The boxes would have been too heavy and awkward to carry and suspicious looking. Each mule carried one hundred gingerbread dolls, fifty on each side of their saddlebag each mule had a search member with it and the plan was to evacuate the slot canyon, move in one mule at a time with their search partner and swap the gingerbread dolls around. Catherine knew the slot canyon well and advised the set up of the operation.

They had to hide a lot of men and mules which was the main problem, and they also had to ensure that the inhabitants of the target slot canyon and their helpers moved far away enough from the operation as possible.

Catherine said there was another slot canyon a few feet from Fanny's slot canyon, the men could hide in there, and if the mules were outside they would not look suspicious because a convoy of mules in the Canyon was a very normal sight.

They walked together looking just like a hiking group not at all suspicious. Every time they stopped for a drink, Slick confirmed the plans of the operation with them again. As they drew nearer to the site of the operation they were all very nervous but ready to go. Catherine led the men to the second slot canyon which was about twenty feet away from Fanny's, the men hid inside while the mules stood outside, Slick, Willie and Jane also waited inside. Spike and Butt were to go with Catherine because they had an extremely important role to play.

Catherine showed the men where the slot canyon hideout was, they were told not to move until they saw the inhabitants of the cave running down the creek. Catherine would be the last one running behind them to indicate that no one else was left in the slot canyon.

Catherine, Spike and Butt headed towards the target, Butt was impressingly quiet and light on his hooves, when they arrived they went to the top end of the slot canyon where Fanny and Al generally were. They waited and waited, Fanny and Al had to be inside the hideout before they could make their move, and Catherine decided to help matters along a little as they could not wait all day.

She headed for the bottom end of the hideout and pushed some of the gingerbread dolls over, this made a huge crashing sound and the squirrels darted around everywhere trying to put them back before Fanny saw them. Catherine scurried back to Spike and Butt, just in time to see Fanny and Al enter the hideout to see what was going on.

Catherine signalled for Butt and Spike to do their job, Spike ran to the top entrance of the slot canyon and stood with his bottom end pointing inwards, he let out the biggest smelliest fart his little body could muster, his abdomen sucking in and out with the effort he was putting in. The smell was horrendous but that was the point.

Butt did his job; he stood on each of the ovens and crushed them completely destroying them. The stench in the slot canyon was so bad there was a mass exodus everyone scrambled to get out, Fanny and Al were surrounded by hundreds of squirrels, the opening to the hideout was becoming a bottle neck with bodies fighting for freedom and fresh air. Eventually they all escaped. Catherine was sure no one would be left behind the smell was enough to make your eyes bleed.

There was a thundering sound as hundreds of feet ran down the creek; they knew they would have to run a long way to get away from the smell. Fanny and Al ran too, Al stopped and threw up twice while making good his escape. Catherine came running down a few seconds later indicating to Slick that it was time to go in.

Slick gave the signal and the first of the men and mules headed up towards the hideout, the men were wearing masks because of the smell and gloves because of the poisonous gingerbread dolls, the mules had tea tree oil rubbed under their noses. With precision and excellent organisation, the gingerbread dolls were swapped around within fifteen minutes.

Butt and Spike had made their way down to the bottom end of the hideout where Butt praised his fellow mules for their work. Spike went through the slot canyon with Catherine to make sure nothing looked abnormal for when the outlaws returned.

With everything in order, they moved towards Phantom Ranch. On the way they passed a few squirrels which were washing in a small pool, they were trying to wash the smell from their fur. Catherine jumped up onto Slick and hid in his back pack so they didn't see her. The rest of the squirrels, Fanny and Al had made their way to a waterfall where they could shower the smell off. Willie and Jane remained covert too by hiding in the back packs of two of the searchers. If Fanny or Al should see them it would blow the operation.

The group kept a steady pace and arrived back at Phantom a few hours later, Slick had not radioed in he didn't want the outlaws to hear him. When they returned to Phantom they were welcomed, the officer in charge new they would be arriving soon because he knew his guys were excellent at their job. He told everyone to go to the canteen and grab a drink and something to eat.

The gingerbread dolls were offloaded this was organised by Budd who had stayed behind to arrange the packaging of the gingerbread dolls for the purpose of evidence. They were placed in bags as they came out of the mule's saddlebags in groups of fifty and labelled. A huge pot of coffee was placed on a big table in the canteen and they were all served up a meal of pancakes, ham, beans and maple syrup.

For the next few days it was a waiting game, no one knew when Fanny and Al were going to make their move towards the popular view points. Catherine ate some food and headed back to Bright Angel Creek, she was given a radio by the officer in charge and told to hide it in a safe place he told her to radio Willie as soon as there was any sign of movement from the outlaws, of course humans could not understand her language. She felt good; she had played a very important part in this operation and had enjoyed every second.

When they had finished their food and coffee Jane and Willie went for a walk down to the river, they had been through a lot the last few weeks and just needed some time together to sit and talk about what had happened. Jane was deeply affected by Ma Cahill's death and was glad she didn't have to go anywhere near Fanny, she felt that if she did she would smash her into crumbs. Because she was here hunting for Fanny she had to leave Baby and Floating Cloud and she missed them. They would have been a comfort to her at this time, and so would being at home in their little house.

Catherine
the secret
agent squirrel

Willie tried to cheer her up a bit he told her to think of the good times they had with Ma Cahill and the way she took care of them and taught them everything she could to give them the best start in life. Jane tried to smile but still felt very sad.

Suddenly they could hear something, it was a beautiful voice singing and it was floating towards them Willie stood up and looked upstream. It was Ichee in a boat, he was singing his head off he looked very happy and content.

Ichee steered the boat towards the bank, got out and tied it to a rock. He walked to the back of the boat and took out a small wooden box with four wheels and a handle attached to it. Willie and Jane excitedly ran towards him to greet him. Then they saw Becci getting out of the boat she looked very well Canyon life obviously suited her.

Then Becci reached down to the bottom of the boat and lifted up a soft white blanket which was then carefully handed to Ichee, he took the blanket and gently placed it into the wooden contraption.

Jane wondered what it was that Ichee was being so careful with, when she arrived at the boat Becci and Ichee where both standing on the shore.

Becci smiled widely when she saw them both and Ichee was thrilled to see them. Jane was curious and desperately wanted to have a look in the wooden box; Becci could see Jane's curiosity and told her to take a look. Jane looked into the box, she couldn't see anything just the soft fluffy white blanket, she put her hand in and pulled the blanket to one side, what a surprise wrapped in the blanket were three of the most beautiful, fluffy, cute babies she had ever seen, Jane burst into tears, what a wonderful sight to behold after so many sad things had happened. Jane gave Becci and Ichee a big hug and congratulated them.

Becci introduced her newborn kittens to Jane and Willie. They had been blessed with two little boys named Alex and Joseph and a little girl named Lara. Ichee and Becci were very proud parents and doted on their babies who were just one week old. They had been staying at Becci's parents home when the kittens had been born, so had no idea what had been going on in the Canyon.

Willie explained about Fanny and what had happened including the death of Ma Cahill. Becci was very sorry she couldn't believe anyone could be so evil.

Once Willie had told them everything and brought them up to date with what was happening, they walked up to the canteen to get something to eat and some coffee. Jane was very happy when Becci said she could push the babies in their little carriage, she had instantly fallen in love with them.

Becci told Jane that she wanted to go to Grand Canyon Village within the next few days to get some supplies, and asked Jane if she would like to join her to help her with the babies, Ichee had to stay behind to make some minor alterations to their home now that the kittens had arrived. Thinking it would be a lovely way to catch up with Becci and get to know the kittens, Jane thought it was a wonderful idea.

A few hours after Catherine's return to the slot canyon, the outlaws also arrived they hadn't noticed that the gingerbread dolls had been swapped. Fanny was furious about her ovens, and blamed it on Canyon mules, which was not too far from the truth she had also decided that there was no need to set up anymore ovens because she had enough gingerbread dolls to do what she wanted to do.

Catherine helped Fanny clear up the mess left from the smashed ovens so she could try and extract as much information from her as possible using the open question "Ted the Spider" technique. She found out that Fanny and Al were to make each squirrel carry ten gingerbread dolls to the rim within the next few days. They would all be provided with a backpack to put them in. Catherine knew this would be a struggle for them as the squirrels were small and the gingerbread dolls were about the same size as them.

Catherine asked Fanny if she minded her suggesting something which may be a little easier. Fanny looked at Catherine with a sly look and an evil glint which made her feel very uneasy, she thought Fanny may have sensed what she was up to. Then surprisingly Fanny asked Catherine what her idea was, she realised that Catherine could actually be an asset to her, also with her being female she may be better to work with.

Catherine realised this was her opportunity to reel Fanny in and get her to tell her more by creating trust between them. she explained to Fanny that if the squirrels carried the dolls all the way to the rim there was a good chance they would lose a lot of them because the squirrels would be struggling, it would be much better if they floated the dolls down the river and then the squirrels could take them up and down the trail, they could make a few trips each so the dolls would not be too heavy. For them to carry them through the Canyon then up the trail would create more risk to damage and loss.

Fanny looked at Catherine, she could see her point and see could see that it was a very good idea. She went inside the slot canyon with Catherine and told the other squirrels that they were to build a boat out of wood which they had to find, they also had to take orders from Catherine as she was in charge of the preparation of the boat and the transport of the dolls to the Bright Angel Trail. When Fanny thought about this, she realised it was a smart move, they would have to pass Phantom Ranch and a load of squirrels struggling with gingerbread dolls may look highly suspicious, but if they were in a boat covered over, no one would know anything about them.

She needed the squirrels to be fit and well rested for the trips they would need to make to the rim, so they would also ride in the boat and keep their heads low. Catherine sent fifty squirrels out looking for any wood they could find to make the boat, she told the rest of the squirrels to prepare the ground near the creek as a work area for building the boat and to gather as much material as they could find which may assist in the construction of it.

Catherine had a way of keeping everyone busy, this way she was in complete control of the situation and they had no time to question anything she asked them to do. She gave them breaks at regular intervals to create trust in her and keep their moral and work quality in excellent condition, firm but fair she ran an excellent work force.

While controlling the boat building process, she kept in regular contact with Willie via the radio to keep them informed at Phantom Ranch. The squirrels that had gone to search for wood returned sooner than expected and brought with them a surprise, they had found a damaged boat which looked like it had been abandoned at the Phantom Creek confluence with Bright Angel Creek, Catherine was impressed and asked Fanny to come and have a look at it. Fanny was pleased, this meant they had a head start the boat did have a bit of damage to it but it could be repaired and that would be a much quicker option than building one from scratch.

Al inspected the boat and said it would take a few hours to get it patched up and water tight, for once he offered to do something to help rather than laze about hiding in the slot canyon; he thought it would be an interesting project. Al was looking forward to giving out the dolls as much as Fanny was, he knew he was wanted, but he thought that if he wore a disguise no one would know any different. While she had been working for El Tovar, Fanny had stolen a Harvey Girl uniform for Al to wear and a curly wig which she took from the room of a lady visitor, he looked good in the uniform, although it was slightly worrying to Fanny that he wore it more often than he needed to.

Work started on the boat and Catherine praised her work force and encouraged them to work faster, Al and Fanny found her fairness to people strange as fair was not a concept they were familiar with, but they could see how it worked to get the job done quicker, and were reluctantly impressed. The boat was finished within four hours and launched onto the water, it floated and there were no leaks. Fanny wanted to start her operation the next morning, there was no point in hanging around, Catherine agreed and told her they should prepare for their journey that night so they could make an early start in the morning, that way they could get all the dolls up onto the rim by the end of the evening and target many more people by starting early the next day.

She gave orders that all the dolls were to be stacked in batches of fifty and evenly distributed across the bottom of the boat, the squirrels were to sit around the edges of the boat leaving room for Fanny and Al at the back. She asked Fanny and Al if they were happy with the plans, they said they were very impressed with her and the way she had motivated the army. She told them there were a few fine details she wished to go over on her own and asked them if they minded her retiring to bed early. Catherine made herself comfortable in the nearby slot canyon where the search team had hidden; she had stashed her radio in there along with some food she had brought from Phantom. She was very hungry so settled down for some well earned food and a good rest.

CHAPTER NINETEEN

In the darkness of her slot canyon with a nice full belly, Catherine radioed Willie. She told him what had happened that day and about the plans Fanny and Al had made for transporting the dolls and distributing them to the unsuspecting Canyon visitors. Willie translated the whole of the operation Fanny and Al had planned to Slick who made a full written report to submit to the leading search team officer.

They had to gather as much evidence as possible to make a firm prosecution, after all almost all evidence so far was hearsay. The dolls were the only solid evidence, but in order for criminal intent to be proven Fanny and Al had to be seen committing the act, stopping them before they did so was not an option.

The team were very proud of Catherine she had done well so far. That evening they were all a little happier because it seemed the plans were coming together and they had a more relaxed evening. Butt was his usual self drinking his Star Butts and acting crazy, and Spike decided to join in with him, he tried some moonshine and started to laugh uncontrollably this worried Willie because the local police were familiar with moonshine but the search team weren't and they may get into trouble if caught with it, because of this they all went to Jane's cabin.

They took some food with them, Willie had only managed to bring two bottles of moonshine with him because that was all he could carry in his back pack without it being noticed, but he knew he would have enough to keep them going because this batch was a strong one, he had hidden it under a bush when they had gone to seek out Fanny and Al at Bright Angel Creek, and was very pleased to still find it there upon his return.

Jane put all the food they had onto a small table. It was getting a little cold so they lit the log fire, it was very cosy. Spike was lying in front of the fire sleeping off his first encounter with moonshine he was dreaming of something, he was whimpering and growling his legs were air running indicating he was chasing something in his dream or being chased by something else. It was very funny to watch especially as when his nose twitched his glasses slid down and he unknowingly pushed them back up with his tongue.

Butt who was laying flat out on the floor near the door was licking his hooves, he liked to remove the red sandstone dust off them at the end of everyday because it gave him something to do and it felt good grinding it between his teeth, a habit he had only recently picked up through boredom. Ichee and Becci were invited to stay with the babies and they settled them down in the bedroom.

Willie made a pot of coffee for everyone and they sat and talked. Butt was getting restless and Willie knew it was because he could see the moonshine but it was in the bottle and not in his coffee so he poured some into his mug. Ichee looked on with interest, receiving a firm elbowing from Becci and a look which would turn milk sour. Butt didn't like drinking alone when he had company, because it was not often he had company. Willie was compelled to join him.

Jane didn't approve of moonshine but Willie and Butt were individuals and grownups, so she couldn't tell them what to do besides the moonshine thing had become a bit of a ritual with them. Willie drank his neat and Butt drank his in his coffee until the coffee ran out, then he went to the neat stage, they both giggled and laughed over the most stupid things.

Willie asked Jane to pass the peanuts from the table and he put them on the floor for him and Butt to share, he couldn't get up and get them himself because he had spaghetti legs.

They thought it would be fun to play a game where one of them threw a peanut and the other one had to catch it, they had to stay in the sitting position because of the leg deadness which would make it funnier and probably safer, having a mule in your sitting room drunk on moonshine and chasing peanuts was a massive safety risk.

Ichee was so desperate to join in the fun he was fidgeting and huffing, Becci felt a bit mean and told him he could have two glasses of moonshine and no more, she was going to bed to get some sleep before the babies woke for their next feed. Jane decided to go to the bedroom too and told Becci she would help her with the babies when they woke.

When the girls had gone the fun began, Butt told Willie to continue with the nut throwing, the rule was not to move your legs which they couldn't anyway, just your body and the nut had to land directly into the mouth. Willie threw five nuts and Butt caught every one of them.

Butt couldn't throw because he didn't have any fingers so he dipped his nose into the nuts with great concentration and flipped a nut into the air. Willie caught it he had to catch another four to match Butt. Ichee wanted a go so he drank a glass of moonshine to get him in the mood, by the time he had downed his first glass, it was his turn to catch the nuts. Willie threw them and he also managed to get five of them in his mouth without a problem, of course the moonshine always seemed to affect the bottom half of the body before the top half.

Willie passed the bottle of moonshine around and they topped up, Ichee felt a bit short changed as his glass was a shot glass and Willie and butt were using tin mugs, Willie gave him a bigger glass, Ichee felt guilty but as Butt pointed out, Becci said he could have two glasses but she had not said which size the glasses should be. Thinking that was a reasonable argument, Ichee accepted the larger glass and filled it to the top.

It was Butt's turn to catch the nuts and Ichee said he wanted to throw them for him, he grabbed five nuts and Butt had a quick mouthful of moonshine then sat up in the waiting position. Ichee threw the first nut, Butt caught it when he clapped his mouth shut it made a loud click as his teeth slapped together, for some reason this set Ichee off into hysterical laughter he tried to throw the next nut but it missed Butt and flew towards the door hitting it with a bang, Butt still went for the nut and toppled backwards, once he had gone past the point of no return he threw his legs around desperately to maintain his balance he had no chance, he did a backward roll and ended up in the corner upside down with his head between his front legs.

His hind legs were balancing precariously he struggled to maintain the position in the hope one of his friends would come to his assistance.

Neither Ichee nor Willie could move, they were both pissing themselves laughing, they tried to wake Spike for him to get Jane but Spike was out of it completely. Slowly Butt started to lose his position, his back end was so heavy it was pushing forward bending his neck and he panicked thinking his neck was going to break and wiggled around in fright. Suddenly he toppled over Willie quickly threw a couple of cushions onto the floor to break his fall, mainly because he knew they would be in trouble with Becci and Jane if they made too much noise. Butt landed safely but as he did he knocked Ichee's arm, and flicked the remaining nuts into the air unbelievably he caught them in his mouth.

Willie laughed so much he couldn't breathe Ichee rolled about trying to stifle his laughter, as he rolled about he squashed Spike's tail, Spike woke up because of the pain in his tail and as he went to yelp, Ichee put his paw over his mouth, Spike bit Ichee's paw and Ichee let out the longest verse of filthy words anyone could think of. Everyone went silent, Willie couldn't believe it, for the first time since the mouth and soap incident Ichee had said a string of naughty words, Willie felt terrible, he felt responsible for making Ichee swear and break his promise to Becci and Jane.

Spike had no idea what was going on, he looked on in confusion. For a few minutes the four of them sat and looked at each other. When there was no movement from the bedroom and they realised Ichee had got away with it, Willie topped everyone up with moonshine and they made a pact never to tell anyone what Ichee had done.

Spike was given a small amount of moonshine because he was only small, and Willie didn't want anything to happen to him, he liked it, the second glass didn't seem as bad as the first, Butt asked him if he wanted to play the nut game, Willie wasn't sure if this was a good idea, but Butt said they would be more careful this time and it was only fair that Spike had a go.

Reluctantly Willie agreed. Spike sat up and waited, Willie said he would throw the nuts for Spike, Ichee and Butt watched. Willie threw the first nut, Spike caught it, and his mouth snapped shut. Willie threw the second nut, he caught it and his mouth snapped shut. Deep in his belly Butt could feel a giggle erupting, it was the mouth snapping shut which was getting to him because not only was the noise funny, but Spike's face was too, when the nut approached, he went cross eyed, and his eyes were magnified by his specs. It looked like he didn't like the taste of the nuts too, they were a bit too salty so each time he caught one he wrinkled his nose up and pushed his tongue between his teeth making a squishy sound.

Butt tried to tell Willie to stop because he was finding it too funny to watch, but he couldn't because the giggle was beginning to surface. Willie threw the nut, and spike caught it in the same way. Butt let out a laugh which was indescribable; it was like someone blowing down a corrugated plastic tube, but with a massive eeeeeeeeaaaaaaaaawwwwwww mixed in with it.

Spike jumped about two feet into the air, because of the loudness of Butt's laugh, as he jumped he let out a huge fart, but also had the misfortune of shooting a huge moonshine covered poo into the fire which exploded into flames and glowed bright blue. Ichee and Willie lost it at this point and both collapsed onto the floor gasping for breath.

What an evening of events, Butt and Spike were now sitting in the upright position, both of them laughing in the same way with their gums pulled over their teeth and hissing, their tongues slightly showing between their teeth. Willie made the mistake of looking at them both as they uncannily laughed in an identical way, Butt laughing like this always set him off but to see both of them doing it simultaneously was just too much, Willie pissed all over the floor.

How they didn't wake Becci and Jane was a mystery, they soon got to the point when they physically couldn't laugh anymore. Willie was rather embarrassed about his accident and had sobered up a little, he had spaghetti legs still and wondered how he was going to get to the bathroom, then he realised that was the least of his problems, where he had been travelling in the backpack of one of the search officers, his bottom had been rubbing on the edge of a match box and had scratched away some of his varnish, his bottom was now soggy and getting out of shape. He had to get to the fire before his bottom fell off; it was just like a biscuit when it breaks off in your tea when you are dunking it.

Butt could see what was happening he got a cushion from the sofa and pushed Willie onto it, he pulled him bottom first in front of the fire, unfortunately for Willie he had to let Ichee remove his trousers so they could expose his bum to the heat, luckily none of him had fallen away into his trousers.

As he was on all fours on the cushion with his bum in the air and Ichee was pulling off his trousers, Spike and Butt were looking on. It was very unfortunate that Jane happened to walk into the room at that moment, her jaw dropped. Ichee and Butt both struggled to explain what was happening but the words wouldn't come out.

Jane walked over to Willie to see what the hell was going on, then she saw the problem, she was disgusted that Willie had drunk so much moonshine that he had pissed his pants but also knew he needed to get dry, she tried her best to push his bottom back into shape as it dried so it wasn't too bad a shape. When it was dry she varnished it, unfortunately for Willie he had to stay in that position until the varnish had dried so that he didn't get any cracks in his bottom, other than the ones which were supposed to be there.

No one wanted more moonshine for some reason and settled down to sleep, Butt slept near the door, Spike lay near the fire next to Willie and Ichee slept on the chair. Jane went back to the bedroom to check on Becci and the babies; Becci was not feeling well she had done too much after having the babies and was exhausted.

The next morning they were all a bit hung over, Willie was stiff from being in the same position all night but his back end was dry and actually it was a much better shape more rounded and tight. Butt was ok because he was used to it, Ichee was a bit wobbly, Spike kept hitting out with his front paws as though he was trying to shoo a fly away, there was nothing there, just the effect of a first moonshine experience.

Becci and the babies were awake, she had fed them and Jane had helped to bath and dry them, they were so cute, Joseph seemed to settle well with Jane which was a great help to Becci because he was the one she had trouble getting off to sleep. Slick knocked at the door and told them to get some breakfast from the canteen; they should always be prepared because they could be called into action at any time.

When they arrived at the canteen, the whole of the search group was there ready to plan their day. Budd told them that all the evil gingerbread dolls had been taken to the rim and were a significant part of the case against Fanny and Al, but it was far from over, everyone had to be vigilant.

In the slot canyon hideout, Fanny and her troops were planning their operation to get the gingerbread dolls to the rim. Al also had the idea that their movements would look less suspicious during the day if they blended in with other Canyon visitors. Fanny was looking quite stressed and she never showed emotion.

Catherine had been up early supervising the last of the stuff from the hideout to the boat, the water levels at Bright Angel Creek were quite high because of the recent flash flood so the boat shouldn't have any problems floating down it.

The boat was ready and Fanny and Al were getting closer to achieving their goal, or so they thought. By10am the boat was launched, all of the squirrels needed for the operation were on board. Fanny was sat at the front and Al, dressed as a Harvey Girl Waitress was sat at the back with the oars. If the situation were not so illegal and serious they would have looked a very funny sight. Catherine told Fanny she would catch them up as soon as she had made sure the hideout was inspected to be certain they had not left any evidence behind. Fanny nodded, very pleased that she had such a thorough and efficient assistant.

As soon as the boat floated away Catherine radioed Willie to tell him Fanny and Al were on the move.

CHAPTER TWENTY

As soon as the signal came from Catherine everyone sprang into action, the search team were very well organised and experienced, the key to the operation was to act as normal as possible and to let Fanny and Al complete their plan so they could get caught and locked away for as long as possible.

The plan which was set into place was very simple, Fanny, Al and their gang were to be followed carefully, the search team knew they would be heading up the Bright Angel Trail and a few of the officers from Phantom would be watching them. At the Rim all the popular lookouts were covered by officers. The roads into the Canyon had been closed and no visitors were allowed in, any visitors already on the rim were told not to go near any of the view points because a police incident was in operation. At Ma Cahill's house the police officers were on standby should Fanny and Al return there for any reason.

Extra officers were brought in from all over the county they were dressed in plain clothes and were to act as visitors at the view points, no member of the public was to come into contact with any of the wanted whether it be man, gingerbread or squirrel.

Willie and Jane went with Slick and Budd again, they waited in a boat on the river near Phantom Ranch, Catherine radioed to tell them that the target boat was at the end of Bright Angel Creek. They waited for the boat to arrive, with Al dressed as a Harvey Girl and the boat fronted by a two foot gingerbread girl they should be quite easy to spot. As they waited they were passed by lots of river runners and people walking.

Bright Angel Trail was closed to visitors, but Fanny and Al had no knowledge of this, again plain clothed officers were to use the trail so things looked normal and they could keep an eye on what the evil pair were up to.

Eventually Slick, Budd, Jane and Willie had to wait no longer the target boat past them. Willie and Jane hid in the bottom of the boat so they would not be seen. Once the boat passed them, Slick and Budd set off after them.

Soon Fanny and her gang arrived to the point where they were to leave the boat and head up the Bright Angel Trail. They considered this the risky part of the trip as they were opposite Phantom Lodge on the confluence of Bright Angel Creek and the Colorado and they were afraid of being seen. Of course no one was going to stop them anyway unknown to them.

Slick, Budd, Willie and Jane would no longer follow them their job for now was done. Fanny was first out of the boat, she ordered the squirrels to off load the gingerbread dolls at once. When they were all loaded onto the shore each squirrel had to line up and was given a backpack, in the pack they had to carry at least three gingerbread dolls each. By this time Catherine had arrived, she knew that the squirrels would struggle with the load they were expected to carry the gingerbread dolls were the same size as the squirrels.

Catherine had a better idea, she had seen two sleeping bags abandoned near the river if they filled the sleeping bags with the gingerbread dolls and the squirrels pulled the bags up the trail they would get the whole lot up the trail quicker and in one trip.

Fanny agreed, she and Al went with Catherine to collect the sleeping bags. When they returned they took great care when placing the gingerbread dolls into the sleeping bags, they tied string around the bags and also attached fifty pieces of string to each bag for the squirrels to pull, Fanny and Al would help to pull the bags too. They crossed the Silver Bridge and headed up The Bright Angel Trail. Once they got going and into a good rhythm they were heading up the trail at good speed.

Catherine went with them and led the way she told Fanny she would go a little further ahead to check there were no potential problems on the trail. Every so often when she was out of sight she used her radio to inform the search teams via Willie of what was happening.

That morning Becci had been looking for Jane after breakfast to go with her to Grand Canyon Village, not being able to find Jane because she had gone in the boat. Becci decided to go to the village with the babies alone as she needed some supplies. She wrapped the babies in a sling around her body, crossed the Kaibab Bridge and headed up the South Kaibab Trail.

When Becci arrived at the village she was very hot and exhausted, she went to El Tovar and ordered herself a cold drink and a sandwich, Emily was on the desk and she was admiring the babies they were hungry by now.

Jane was at Phantom looking for Becci and the babies, she knew they were due a feed and wanted to help. She went back to her cabin expecting Becci to be there but she was gone, the baby cart was still outside so she didn't think she had gone far. Then she saw that the baby blanket was gone, she knew now what Becci had done.

Frantically she ran to Budd and told him about Becci and the babies, Budd immediately called El Tovar to tell them to look out for Becci and not let her out of their sight if they saw her. Emily told him Becci and the babies were there and she would give them a room to rest in and keep them safe.

Relieved, Jane went back to the cabin to rest and pack her things, Budd said he would come and get her when they were ready to leave for Grand Canyon Village.

Fanny, Al and the squirrels reached the top of the trail by 4pm, there was no way Fanny was going to give out the dolls today it was too late and there were not enough victims around. They dragged the sleeping bags under the cover of the trees and made themselves comfortable for the night, Fanny wanted to make sure she affected as many people as possible with her evil plan.

Catherine radioed the plan to Willie. Slick was not surprised by her move and said it suited them better because they could get a good rest and set up early for her the next morning. Catherine went to see Becci to make sure she had everything she needed; she and the babies were to stay at El Tovar until the operation was over. Ichee was very worried about Becci and the babies but Jane told him the staff at El Tovar were lovely and they would be safe and very well looked after.

Catherine had a restless night, she knew Fanny wouldn't start anything without her but she was still anxious. She wanted to make sure she didn't miss out on any detail and put someone in danger.

The next morning a helicopter went into the Canyon to bring Slick, Budd, Jane and Willie out. They were then taken to Grand Canyon Village by bus and when Catherine gave the all clear Willie and Jane went into El Tovar Hotel to hide in safety. Slick and Budd parked up in the car to wait confirmation of Fanny and Al's movements.

At 7am buses arrived at the Canyon intermittently containing the plain clothed officers to act as visitors, the buses stopped off at various view points. At 7.10 Catherine radioed Willie and told him Fanny and Al were ready and had were planning to cover two of the most popular view points, Powell Point and Hopi Point, these points had been chosen because they both protruded out of the rim giving a fantastic and thrilling view of the Canyon.

Fanny, Al and the Squirrels set off to commit their crime. Catherine told Fanny that she was going to head for Grand Canyon Village to tell more visitors that delicious gingerbread dolls were being given away at the two points. Fanny agreed it was a very good idea.

With the officers in place and Fanny and her group en route the operation began. As they dragged the sleeping bags to the two points, it didn't matter if anyone questioned what was in them, because they were filled with innocent gingerbread dolls as far as anyone was concerned. Al was to give out the gingerbread dolls at Powell Point, and Fanny would give them out at Hopi Point, they would both have their Harvey Girl uniforms on so it looked more realistic.

Fanny couldn't wait the thought of seeing total carnage take place was almost bringing a smile to her face. Some of the "visitors" were dropped off at Hopi point then the bus took the remaining ones to Powel Point. Fanny stood at the start of the lookout waiting for her victims. The visitors walked around taking in the spectacular views of the Canyon and breathing in the fresh Canyon air.

From the trees Fanny appeared, she had a basket lined with a checked cloth and the gingerbread dolls were neatly placed in it. Her uniform looked immaculate and she actually looked quite pleasant. She stood at the rim where the visitors would walk out; as they approached her she kindly and sweetly offered them a gingerbread doll biscuit.

One of the female officers took one from the basket; she took a bite and said it was the most delicious gingerbread she had ever tasted. The other visitors came up and helped themselves too, Fanny couldn't believe it, they were almost gone, and at this rate she would have to top up the basket again. At Powell Point Al was doing even better, he had already topped up his basket for the second time.

Just as Fanny and Al were getting to the end of their supply, an officer at each point stepped in and arrested them both for conspiracy to commit mass murder. Al went to run, but he was wrestled to the ground and hand cuffed, a police van came and took him away. The officer arresting Fanny was a female, she had no idea how evil Fanny was or indeed how strong she was, as she went to cuff Fanny, she grabbed the officer and pushed her against a rock. The officer grabbed Fanny and as two other officers came to her assistance, the female fell. She slipped and tumbled down into the Canyon the other officers looked over the edge to see her holding on to a ledge about six feet below them. As they tried to help her, Fanny made good her escape and ran off. The squirrels scattered they didn't want to be associated with Fanny. She was now alone and being hunted. The female officer was pulled to safety and taken to hospital.

Catherine was now at El Tovar and she could hear on the radio what had happened. She was the only one who could find Fanny because Fanny still trusted her. She left El Tovar and headed towards Hopi Point, she told Willie she would get Fanny to come towards Grand Canyon Village.

Unfortunately, Fanny took a route which was unexpected and she arrived at Grand Canyon Village a different way so Catherine didn't see her. Fanny thought that if she went into El Tovar she could take some food and water providing her with some supplies to enable her to go on the run. Just as she was about to leave the kitchen, Becci walked in to get some food for her babies, she had baby Joseph in her arms trying to settle him, she screamed at the top of her voice to let everyone know Fanny was in the kitchen, Willie came running and Slick was behind him. There was a standoff in the kitchen.

Fanny stood perfectly still, she could go out of the back door if she wished but she was afraid there may be more police outside, she picked up everything she could find and threw it towards Willie, Becci and Slick. Pots, pans, knives, forks were hurled at them. One of the pans hit Slick on the head and he fell to the floor unconscious. Willie knelt down on the floor to help Slick.

Fanny headed for the door only to be tripped up by Becci. Fanny was furious, she got back onto her feet and punched Becci in the face, Becci fell to the ground, Fanny immediately bent down picked up her baby and took it away with her. She ran out into the Village carrying baby Joseph, he cried for his mother but she told him to shut up.

Jane was walking from the camp ground and she saw Fanny with Joseph, she begged Fanny to let him go she walked towards her holding out her arms for Fanny to give the baby to her. Fanny just laughed and walked away she headed towards Powell view point, she intended to hitch a ride on the visitors bus, not realising of course that they were all police officers.

Becci regained consciousness, as soon as she realised Joseph was missing she was filled with strength and anger she had never felt before, she was bruised and hurt but she did not feel a thing, she wanted her baby back and she was going to get him back whatever happened.

She asked Emily to look after the other two babies and walked out of the hotel, Jane had been with Budd looking out for Fanny, she saw Becci heading out of the village, she called to her but Becci didn't hear, she was so angry and full of intent she could not hear anyone. But as she walked along what she did hear was the crying of her baby, she followed the cries and saw Fanny, she was sitting on a rock at the edge of the Canyon with Joseph.

Becci stopped dead in her tracks, Fanny held Joseph by the scruff of his neck and dangled him above the rim, the poor furry little guy was suspended a mile above the Canyon by a crazy evil gingerbread bitch. Becci didn't know what to do, if she moved her baby would be dropped to his death. She stood alone in front of Fanny, the wind started to pick up and blow sandstone dust around them.

Fanny knew there was nothing Becci could do and smirked at her, she told Becci that she would only get her baby back if she arranged for her to be transported from the Canyon without any implications; she wanted to go home and make biscuits.

Fanny was obviously deranged, how could she think of going home and making biscuits after all she had done. Fanny started to hum to herself, she had lost the plot, she was humming "Somewhere over the rainbow" just as she came to the second verse, Becci could see something move next to Fanny, it was a snake, a rattle snake, Fanny looked down and saw her good pal Vicious Vicky. Vicky was not looking at Fanny, she was looking at the baby she had dangling over the edge and Becci didn't know what the hell to do her baby was between two evils and a mile drop.

Fanny tried to catch Vicky's attention but she would not take her eyes off the baby. Vicky slowly started to go round and round the rock twisting and turning, Fanny shouted at her to stop she was making her dizzy and was afraid she would fall off the rock.

As Fanny was pleading with Vicky to stop, a huge eagle swooped down from the sky snatched poor little Joseph from Fanny's grip and flew away with him, Becci was distraught and dropped to the floor, Fanny fell off the rock and onto the edge of the rim. Vicky slithered off into the bushes.

Jane arrived just as Becci pulled herself up from the floor, Becci surged forward towards Fanny all she wanted to do was make her hurt, to cause her as much pain as possible she was a mother now and there was no love like a mother's love and no revenge could match what she had in store for Fanny. Becci reached the rock where fanny lay she hit her so hard she knocked her right arm clean off and it flew across the air and down into the Canyon.

Jane called to Becci to stop, she was terrified Becci would end up over the edge and she had to think of her two remaining babies. Becci would not listen, with all of her strength she picked Fanny up off the floor and again punched her hard in the face, this time Fanny just laughed at her

"You can't kill evil" Shouted Fanny

"I will have a damn good go" screamed Becci, One of the phases she had heard Ichee say. She turned her back on Fanny as though she was going to walk away, Fanny laughed at her. With a deep breath and a clenched paw Becci spun around quickly and simultaneously kicked and punched with her right fist and right leg at Fanny launching her into the air and over the edge of the Canyon. She seemed to fly forever then she dropped and she was gone.

Jane looked over the edge she could not see any sign of Fanny, Becci was shaking and crying, she sobbed for her baby, then she sobbed because she thought she would go to jail for murdering Fanny and would have to leave Ichee and her other two babies behind. Just above them a shadow appeared blocking out the sun. Jane looked up and could just make out the shape of a bird; it circled them for a few minutes and then landed a few feet away from them. At the same moment Vicious Vicky appeared, neither Jane or Becci were afraid of her at that moment, she was the least of their worries.

Vicki went up to Becci and gently rubbed against her leg, she also looked at Jane, the black deadness in Vicky's eyes was no longer there they seemed to have life in them now.

The huge bird which had been circling them from above landed, it was the eagle who had stolen baby Joseph, he walked up to Becci and handed her baby to her, he had saved her baby not taken it. Vicky spoke to them, she said she was very sorry for what she had done in the Canyon, she had been suffering from a mental disorder which had now been treated at the vetenary hospital by an animal psychiatrist. She was now feeling much better and had helped them out because she was desperate to do some good in her life. The eagle was her friend and his name was Christopher, he was a good guy.

Becci hugged her baby tightly and he snuggled into her, he didn't seem to be any the worse for his adventure but was hungry, Becci cried happy tears and took him under the shade of a tree to feed him.

Jane gave Christopher a huge hug and gave Vicky one too, she thanked them both very much for what they had done they had been very brave and very kind.

CHAPTER TWENTY-ONE

Jane headed back to El Tovar with Becci and baby Joseph, Emily greeted them with baby Alex and Baby Lara, she had looked after them well and they were both asleep in a little Indian woven basket on top of their blanket. Becci was so pleased to see them; she placed Joseph in the basket next to them.

Willie came back with Slick and Budd, Becci told Slick she was ready to be arrested and she was not sorry for what she had done. Slick told her to go back to her room and rest with her babies; she would not be arrested because you can't technically kill a biscuit which was basically what Fanny was in reality. Slick told her that Ichee was on his way up from the Canyon.

Willie was very angry, he could not believe Fanny could do something so evil to a little baby and its mother, he knew Fanny was gone but he hated her. Budd brought the subject of Fanny's remains up, he said they would have to be found, if an animal or hungry human should eat her there was a possibility the evil would live within the new host. They went back to the place where Fanny had been launched from the rim to analyse where she may have landed, they were joined by experts who located bodies which had fallen from the rim on a regular basis.

They worked out a search area based on the information given to them by Jane and planned the search and evacuation of Fanny's remains. Christopher the eagle said he would help, if he saw the remains he would sit near them until someone arrived to make sure no one ate them. Vicious Vicky said she would go with him, being low to the ground she would be able to see any crumbs which may be scattered.

The professionals didn't think Fanny would have landed in the Colorado, she probably landed on a rocky part of the Canyon possibly towards the wall because although she did appear to project out quite far there had been a keen wind which would have blown her back in and possibly onto a shelf. The search teams told Willie, Jane and everyone else to stay at Grand Canyon Village they were all exhausted and the find may not be too pretty.

Spike and Butt who were still at Phantom volunteered to join the search, Butt knew the Canyon well and Spike had a good sense of sniffing things out, besides Butt hated Fanny with a passion because of the time she stole his place on the raft and sent shivers down his spine just by looking at him. Spike and Butt had become good friends too, at first they had been jealous of each other because they both were playing for Willie's attention, but the last two days together they had fun and they realised they had a lot more in common than just the weird way which they laughed.

The search teams welcomed the help of Spike and Butt and met them at Phantom Ranch. At the village everyone was sat eating food and drinking coffee, Budd and Slick were to stay with them to inform them of what was happening.

Slick was called to reception to a telephone call, when he returned he told Willie and Jane that Al had been charged with the offence of plotting to commit mass murder, and he had also been charged with another murder which was one of the ones he was being hunted for. He told them that a couple of days before Ma Cahill had given him food and coffee, he had murdered a young nurse by the name of Mary James. Mary's body had been found next to the train line just outside the city limits of Flagstaff. They had found skin under Mary's nails and had obtained a DNA profile from the skin, it matched Al's there were also traces of her blood on his clothing when it had been analysed.

Mary's parents had gone through hell because she had been missing for a week before her body was found and because of her death being a murder, her body could not be released until they had gathered enough forensic evidence. Today she was returned home to Chicago with her parents. Jane cried when she heard this it was so sad, how could anyone kill a young nurse and why did he do it. Unfortunately that was a question everyone wanted to know the answer to but only Alwyn Butch Hung knew the answer.

The search team walked all day to the location where they were sure Fanny's remains would have landed, when they arrived Christopher was waiting for them, he had searched the area well and had actually found a few clues, he had an excellent eye for spotting things from the air and had seen something black and shiny so had swooped down and landed.

What he found was creepy and sickening; he had found Fanny's head. The black shiny objects he had seen were her eyes, they looked just as they did when she had been alive and her head had been attached to her body dead and emotionless. Little beads of evil emptiness. One of the search officers put on a pair of gloves and placed the head in a bag.

Christopher told them there was no way any animal in the Canyon would eat Fanny, they could smell the evil and would avoid it even if they were at the point of death through starvation. Humans however, well that would be a different thing they didn't have the same strength in their senses as animals did and they would probably munch on Fanny as soon as they found her.

Now that Fanny's head had been found Christopher said he would fly over the immediate area and find Vicky, she may be sitting on more evidence. The team decided to take a rest and wait for Christopher to come back. He was not long and when he returned he had good news, Vicky had found the rest of Fanny's body and the arm which Becci had hit off her before she had booted her into the Canyon. The arm had landed on a ledge and her body had been found on the Canyon floor not too far from her head. Vicky had stayed between the two body parts to prevent anyone tampering with them until the search team arrived.

They made their way to Vicky and thanked her very much for preserving the crime scene. She told them a few people had approached but she had hissed them off. Butt found it very difficult to trust Vicky and she told him she didn't blame him for feeling like that at all but she hoped they could become good friends over time; she smiled at Spike and told him she thought he was a very nice looking dog, he blushed.

Christopher had to go so bid goodbye to everyone, he had been a big help to the search team and they could not thank him enough.

Later that day they arrived back at Phantom with Fanny's remains. A helicopter came down from the rim to collect the remains and brought Ichee, Becky, and the babies back. They were feeling a lot better now and Ichee took his family back to their little home.

When the remains arrived at the rim a forensic scientist was there to do some tests on them, and they were taken to a tent which had been set up as a temporary laboratory. There was also a news team reporting on the events which had taken place, the story was broadcast all over the world.

After a few hours the forensic scientist had finished her report and was quite disturbed by what she had found. The remains showed that although Fanny had been alive in every sense of the word, because she had not been born in a way which humans would have been born, it made her immortal, she could not die. Although her body was broken, it seemed to be in some sort of suspended animation indicating that at some stage it would come to life again.

She may not be able to use the body as it was because it was in parts but if her parts were to get into the wrong hands or contaminate some other vessel the evil could continue, her DNA was not dead therefore her human part was not dead so technically neither was Fanny. Burying her in any way or cremating her would not work as her spores would contaminate the soil or the air.

This was truly a nightmare, the FBI came and took Fanny's remains, and they would be kept in a glass sealed cabinet in a sealed vault until a solution could be found to destroy her permanently. Willie and Jane didn't know what to feel, she was their sister but they were glad she was gone, there was nothing they could do now anyway.

Sheriff Earl came to take Willie and Jane back home; when he was driving them back he told them that Ma Cahill's death had been unlawful. The moonshine which had killed her had come from a place on the North Rim, a man had been distilling it using a lead radiator valve, he had no idea he had done anything wrong because he had only just started making it. Skippity Jack Moran had heard there was a new distiller about and he immediately knew the deathly error he had made so went to see him.

The guy was dying when Skippity got there because he had just had a tipple of his own lethal moonshine, but he stayed alive long enough to tell him he had sold five bottles of his moonshine to a gingerbread woman and a twisted looking man. The guy had drunk some for the first time that day because he had been to Vegas for four weeks and had not had chance to try it before he went.

The death of the man was painful and long, Skippity did all he could to make him comfortable and called for medical assistance but he died before it arrived. So they had found the source of Fanny's red moonshine and it looked like the case against Fanny was wrapped up but they still had to find out if Al was involved in Ma's Cahill's death or if Fanny had acted alone.

Sheriff Earl also told them that Al was in prison in Phoenix and had been additionally charged with cattle rustling. Hickory Smoke had been caught and confessed to the murder and attempted murder of the owner of the cattle and the sheriff who had tried to stop him. Unfortunately Al and his father were still guilty of their part with the cattle, it was their fault that they were too stupid to realise what they were doing and stupidity on that scale was not seen to be either a reasonable defence or in the realm of mitigating circumstances.

When they arrived home Jane went to see Baby and check on the other animals. They had all been well looked after. A couple of days later Willie and Jane went back to the Rim to collect Spike and bring him home, he had ridden up the South Kaibab Trail on the back of Butt his new best buddy, it had taken them three days to climb the trail because on the way they finished off the bottle of moonshine Willie had left behind on the night of the nut game.

Spike went home with Willie and Jane, Butt went back down the Canyon he would see them in a few weeks because he was going to spend the winter with them at the house.

Catherine had been enrolled with the FBI; they were so impressed with her skills and the part she played in "Operation Baking Soda" she had been taken on immediately, as she was a squirrel she would be in the special branch.

When they arrived back at the house it seemed more welcoming than ever, although without Ma there it would never be the same. Jane made some coffee and sandwiches and they settled down for the evening.

The next morning, Jane decided she would give the house a good clean, she asked Willie if he would give the barn a good sweep and put down the fresh hay, if they worked together they could get it all shiny and fresh by the evening.

Willie and Spike went to the barn to start work Spike and Baby were not much help because they chased each other around the garden playing so Willie got on with the work himself. It was a warm sunny day but there was a slight breeze it was a perfect day for putting the house rugs on the washing line for a beating.

Jane moved all the rugs outside and hung them up; she got a stick and gave each one a good wack to get the dust off. The stitching on one of the rugs was coming undone around the edge so she thought she would mend it while it was on the line, she went to the house for a needle and thread. As she started to unpick the old stitching she could feel something inside the rug and when she looked closer she could see something white, she un picked the rest of the thread and pulled out an envelope it was addressed to a Mrs E Hughes who lived in Canada.

Jane opened the envelope and pulled out a letter it read:

Dear Eve

Did you receive the gingerbread people I sent you the other day? I know this sounds crazy but they were made out of left over dough from three 2ft tall gingerbreads I made to advertise my baking business from the road and they may be alive. It's difficult to explain but they became contaminated with human DNA, please don't eat them until you are sure they are not alive. The three I have are alive and living.

Louise.

Jane was stunned she didn't know what to do, Ma had written this with urgency, but it had not been posted, why?

She thought about it, the letter was obviously written after they had come to life, but why was it stitched inside the rug and not sent? It had to be the work of Fanny, she always offered to send the post but why would she want to stop the letter? The other gingerbreads wouldn't have been evil as they had not been touched by the fugitive so she would not have had anything in common with them.

Jane ran to Willie and showed him the letter, he couldn't believe what he was seeing, and Jane said she was going to call Skippity Jack Moran to see if he knew who the letter was intended for.

Skippity said it was for Ma Cahill's friend Eve they had met years ago when Ma was walking along the rim, she had been with a group of students who Ma had spent the day with. Eve and Louise had got on very well and they wrote to each other for years although they only ever met up when Eve managed to get back to the Canyon. Ma always sent her biscuits as soon as they were baked, because she wanted them to be as fresh as possible when she got them.

Skippity was puzzled too as to why the letter would be hidden, when Jane suggested it could have been Fanny's doing, he was even more puzzled,

"Why would she care if the gingerbreads came to life and . . . . wait a moment" he said,

"Opening up a parcel to release three gingerbread people who had been sealed up for days and then having them suddenly jump out on you would be enough to give you a heart attack, that is what she wanted to do, cause more suffering and misery even hundreds of miles away from where she was, what a bitch"

"I bet she sat there imagining what would happen smirking to herself" said Jane

Willie decided they should contact Eve to see if she was alright. They looked through Ma's telephone numbers to see if they could find one for Eve, they couldn't just the address which they had on the letter. They realised Eve probably didn't have a number or Ma would have called her and not gone to the trouble of writing her a letter especially over something so serious.

There was only one thing for it, Willie and Spike would have to go to Eva they had to make sure she was ok and if her gingerbreads were alive, Jane would have to stay to look after the house and the animals.

Willie was very nervous he had never been away from the Canyon before. He would also not be here when Butt arrived for the winter, Jane reassured him that Butt would be fine and she would make sure he had everything he needed including moonshine which there was plenty of stashed all over the house and barn. Butt would not be leaving until March anyway so they could catch up when Willie returned home.

Skippity had told them he was coming to see them the next day he had some money Ma Cahill had given him to save for her it would come in handy for the trip to Eve. He wanted to see them before Willie went anyway.

Jane found $500 in a tin in the kitchen which Ma had stashed form her baking business, she told Willie to take that for the journey and to be careful with it.

It seemed it was a day of letters that afternoon a letter arrived from Ma's son in Phoenix; it was lovely to hear from him and it made Jane smile.

CHAPTER TWENTY-TWO

While Jane was cleaning the house she took the time to go through Ma Cahill's things, she was very upset but Willie told her that it had to be done. In the letter from her son he had asked for a few of her items to be sent to him in Phoenix, he only wanted certain things and said they could hold on to everything else. He also wrote that he would try and visit soon and bring Michael with him, this cheered Jane up because she liked Luke Junior a lot and would love to meet Michael.

Jane carefully wrapped and packed all of the things on the list and they were posted off. She laid all the other things belonging to Ma on the table in the lounge and looked at them. Ma had lots of photos and little objects which didn't seem to be very significant to Jane but would have been to Ma or she wouldn't have kept them.

As she looked at the collection she realised they knew very little about her life when she was younger, they really only knew her for who she was when they were created and up until the time she died which was only about seven months in all.

This made Jane feel sad, they did have good memories of her but she had never asked Ma anything about her life and now she wished that she had. As promised, Skippity Jack Moran rode up in his cart pulled by his mule Delilah; it was the first time he had visited since Ma had died. Jane invited him into the house and made a pot of coffee, she put some shortbread biscuits on a plate for Skippity Jack too.

Skippity Jack saw Ma Cahill's belongings on the table and smiled; he recognised a lot of the items and knew what they represented. Jane saw him smile and asked him if he could share some of his memories with them. Skippity said he would be delighted to and it was probably fitting that they knew all he knew about her life.

Jane went to the barn to get Willie who was feeding and watering the animals including Delilah. When they both returned, they topped up their coffee and Skippity started to tell them the story of Ma Cahill.

"She was born in Arizona in September 1968, and was the only daughter of Ann and Anthony Cahill; they also had two sons, Daniel and Elijah. She was very close to her mother and brothers and they loved each other very much, but her father was a bully who drank and gambled most of their money away. She was not allowed to go to school; her father believed it was a waste of time because she would waste an education being a wife and mother. Her mother desperately wanted a better life for her; she didn't want her to end up like her, trapped in a loveless marriage with a controlling bully.

Louise was strong willed however and had no intention of being chained to a house and a husband, her father had already chosen a husband for her a man named Richard Head and Louise hated him, he was fifty two years old and was a drinker and a heavy smoker, he smelt bad and thought he was too rich to be bothered with things like washing himself.

The only reason her father insisted she married Richard was because he had money, also Anthony Cahill owed him a huge gambling dept which would be paid off by giving him his daughter. Louise wasn't interested in money it meant nothing to her.

Often Richard would call in and drink with her father until the early hours of the morning. Louise would have to get up at 5am and Richard would demand she washed him, he was a dirty old man, he would stand in the bath and she had to sponge him down, he said it was good practice for when they were married.

Louise then had to walk three miles to his home, cook and clean for him and walk home. Louise just did as she was told; she knew she was going to get herself away from there. Thanks to her mother, she did learn to keep a good house and she soon became a wonderful cook and baked the best cakes and biscuits for miles. She and her mother would bake and sell their produce to support the family if they didn't they would have starved, they had to hide the money or Anthony Cahill would have spent it on drink.

Every night when Louise went to bed, she would read by candlelight, she taught herself to read because no one else would and she had no schooling, within six months she was reading books which the kids at the local school would not come in contact with for another five years, she was naturally very clever and gifted.

It was August and soon it would be her birthday, she would be sixteen, she hated her birthdays but now she knew this one would be worse because when she was sixteen she would be forced to marry Richard. Her mother didn't want her to marry him either but she couldn't go against her husband as he was very strong willed and when he drank he would get violent. Louise hated to see her mother get a beating and she knew she had to do something soon to get away, but she was terrified her mother and brothers would be punished if she left.

One afternoon Louise went for a walk along the rim, she loved the Canyon so much but she knew she would have to leave to escape her forced marriage to Richard.

While she was walking she came across a group of students from Phoenix, they were having great fun joking and laughing with one another. Louise smiled at them as she walked past and one of the girls said hello to her and introduced herself, her name was Eve.

Louise stopped and spoke to them, when they asked her where she was from and she told them she lived at the Canyon they were fascinated and Eve said she was very lucky. They asked her if she wanted to join them, they were going to have a study afternoon and would value her knowledge of the Canyon very much.

Louise was very pleased that someone was interested in what she had to say she spent the whole afternoon with them and had a wonderful time. They asked her what her school was like and she looked embarrassed, she told them she educated herself because her father didn't allow her to go to school, and she told them about her forced marriage to a fifty two year old man who she hated named Richard Head.

Eva started to cry she felt very sorry for Louise and could not believe she had to do something so terrible. One of the boys pointed out that you could shorten Richards name to Dick and this made them all laugh. Louise had to have it explained to her but thought it was very funny and she would look at him in a different light from now on just because of the alternative name.

The afternoon she had spent with the group had made her realise how much she wanted to live her life her way, she felt a deep sense of determination in her gut, she had captivated them with her knowledge and stories of the Canyon and enjoyed it. Inspired she made her way home.

When she got home her mother was waiting for her, she told Louise to go into the kitchen, when she did she handed her an envelope containing her passport and $500. Her mother Anne told her to take the money and get as far away from her father and Richard as she could, she advised her to go to Phoenix and get herself a good job. Louise started to cry, she told her mother she was worried what may happen to her if she left her alone with her father, her brothers were nine and ten and they could not protect her. Her mother hugged her and said she would be fine, she told her to go and pack her things, leave the house and not look back.

Louise hated the thought of leaving the Canyon but knew it would always be there waiting for her.

Early the next morning she boarded the bus and set off for Phoenix. When she arrived she booked into a hotel for the night.

The next morning she woke feeling refreshed and hungry, she went to the dining room for breakfast and while she was eating, a news report came on the television. A house on the south rim of the Grand Canyon was on fire and the fire was threatening to spread and cause mass damage to the immediate surroundings. It was Louise's house, her heart stopped her first thought was for her mother and brothers. She knew her father had done this because she had left.

She had to go home her mother and brothers needed her. After being in Phoenix for less than twenty four hours she left the hotel and headed back to the Canyon; the journey seemed to take forever as all sorts of worries went through Louise's mind; she had no idea if her mother and brothers were alive or dead. She didn't care much about her father.

When she arrived at the house it was total chaos, there were fire appliances and police cars everywhere, the fire had been put out and there was no longer any danger of it spreading. Louise ran to a police officer who was guarding the scene and asked where the family were. He told her they were safe and they had been taken to El Tovar Hotel, they had not been in the house when the fire had started so were not injured in any way, just needed a place to sleep and rest. Louise was so relived, she went to El Tovar.

Louise entered El Tovar. Her mother and brothers were sat in the dining room being looked after by the staff, they looked fine, her mother was very pleased to see her but also cross with her for coming back and not escaping.

Her mother took her to the privacy of the room they had been given and told her what had happened.

Anthony Cahill had returned home drunk and asked where Louise was, Richard was waiting outside to see her he had a gift for her. Her mother said that Louise was out walking and if he left the gift she would give it to her when she returned. Anthony got angry and said Richard wanted to show Louise what to expect on her wedding night so it was only her who could receive the gift.

At the thought of this her mother lost her temper for the first time in her life and told him that Louise had gone and was never coming back. He was furious and went to hit her, as he raised his left arm, Anne took a pot of hot coffee from the stove and threw it all over him as he rolled around on the floor in agony, she went to the wardrobe and took out his shot gun.

She woke the boys and told them to get out of the house and run like hell, they were terrified and didn't want to leave their mother, but she screamed at them to go. They ran as fast as they could and hid in the forest. Richard came into the house and came face to face with Anne wielding the shot gun, as he turned to run she aimed and shot Richard in the right buttock, he ran out of the house screaming like a girl. Anne was not done yet, she went into the kitchen where Anthony was laying on the floor, she walked up to him and with a strength she never knew she had, she told him to get up and start walking,

"You crazy bitch" he said "This is my house and you will do as I say, now Anne put the god dammed gun down"

Anne was in no mood for reasoning, she had found the strength from somewhere to confront this bully and with a gun in her hand she was for once in her life in control, she told him to get up off the floor and walk out of the door, he slowly got to his feet and walked out of the kitchen, as he passed her he tried to grab the gun off her but she hit him hard in the nuts with the butt of the rifle and he doubled over in pain. Bent over, he struggled towards the door and found his way out.

As he struggled to stand upright, she went behind him pushing him along with the gun, Richard was rolling about on the ground in agony but she showed no mercy, she went over to him and shot him in the left buttock telling him that was from Louise, this severed the femoral artery and he consequently bled to death. Leaving Richard on the ground she continued to push her husband forward with the gun in his back.

They went towards the Canyon all the way he tried to reason with her, but this woman was scorned, she had flipped after years of torment and bullying. When they got to the rim of the Canyon, he was terrified and asked her if they could talk about it, she said yes and they sat near the rim, out of her pocket she took a small bottle of moonshine which she had acquired recently, wiping the bottle on her skirt, she handed it to him.

He immediately opened it and drank the whole lot in one mouthful. As soon as he did, he started to cough and splutter; he coughed up blood and keeled over on the edge of the rim. Anthony pleaded with Anne to help him; she looked down on the pathetic life form and smiled. She wiped the gun over with her skirt, wrapped his hand around the trigger and placed his fingers over the rest of the gun. She did help him though, dying from red moonshine was a slow and painful death, so she put her foot under his hunched up pain riddled body and kicked him over the edge of the Canyon sending him on the one mile journey to his death.

She then made her way back to the house and set it alight she wanted to get rid of everything which reminded her of the life she had with him, she wanted to burn the memories away. She found her boys and they made their way to El Tovar where she called the sheriff.

Louise knew what had happened but no one else did, the sheriff who arrived was new to the job, he said his name was Earl. While the fire crews were fighting the fire, he spoke with Anne and told her she was very lucky to be alive and so were her children. Anne told him that she ran from the house with her boys because her husband was threatening her with a shot gun and he had already shot his friend Richard because they had an argument over a gambling debt which he owed him.

The sheriff said they had found Richards body outside the house but had not found her husband's she told Sheriff Earl that he had headed towards the Canyon rim.

They all stayed at El Tovar that night and the following morning returned to the remains of the house. The whole of the community felt sorry for Anne and everyone brought something for them, luckily the barn was not damaged so they were able to set up home there.

A few days later, Sheriff Earl came to tell them that Anthony's body had been located at the bottom of the Canyon just below Yaki point. His remains had been brought to the rim and taken away for an autopsy which concluded that he had died due to injuries sustained by the fall. He also had red moonshine in his stomach contents so may have lost his mind and thrown himself over the edge after drinking it not knowing it was contaminated. It looked likely he had got the red moonshine from Richard Head as they had found a few bottles of it in his barn.

Over the next few weeks they built a new house, it didn't take long because so many people wanted to help. Soon the house was ready for them to move in. Over the next few months the family's life improved in many ways and they were always smiling, the boys did brilliantly at school and managed to recapture some of their childhood. Louise helped her mother around the house and they made sure the atmosphere and environment was always pleasant and cheerful.

One afternoon Louise was in the garden when a young man drew up on his horse, he introduced himself as Luke and he was trying to find his way to Grand Canyon Village, he was a lecturer and had lost his way. He looked very hot and tired, Louise said she would show him the way but first he should have something to eat and drink.

He smiled at her and climbed down from his horse. She remarked that he didn't have much in the way of luggage with him. He explained that it had been sent on before him and he didn't need much as he was only staying for one week.

Anne was in the kitchen and came out to welcome Luke. She spoke to him while Louise made some coffee and pancakes. While they were eating, Luke asked Louise where she was educated. She told him that she had educated herself at home and she had no formal qualifications but could read, write and had good general knowledge. He asked her if she had good knowledge of the Canyon, Anne interrupted and said Louise's knowledge of the Canyon was excellent because of the passion she had for it.

This interested Luke and he asked her if she would like to join him on his lecture, he needed someone to help him present his subject and he was sure she could do it.

Louise was amazed and accepted the offer, her mother was thrilled and told Luke that she knew her daughter would be a great help to him. Luke's lecture was on Geology, Louise knew nothing about it but apparently that didn't matter he wanted to lecture people on the Canyon from a Geologist point of view and then wanted them to hear about the Canyon from the point of view of someone who lived there and loved it with a passion. A comparison between the scientific approach and human love for the place. He told her he would pay her for her time.

Louise was thrilled, she knew she could do it because she had done it with the students and it had gone well. Luke told her he would be staying at Grand Canyon Village and would meet her there the next day at 8am she gave him directions to the village and off he went.

Louise was thrilled and so was Anne, Louise packed what she needed including a tent and prepared her horse "Star" ready to ride to the Canyon the next morning. When she arrived Luke was waiting for her, he had coffee and pancakes for them in return for the ones she had made him the day before. He explained that he had a group of students who had paid to come on the course from all over the country, there were twenty of them in total, he wanted Louise to just be herself and tell them of the Canyon how she saw it.

They had a fantastic day, their combination of both experiences and knowledge lightly and professionally bounced off each other and the students were captivated by their performance. Luke was thrilled that the day had gone so well and knew the week of lectures would be brilliant.

Louise was a natural, the way she described her environment was honest and child like but beautifully explained. During one of the lectures, a park ranger was present and he was amazed by the way she was able to put into words how she saw and felt the Canyon. When the lecture was finished the Ranger asked Louise if she would be interested in talking to visitors a few times a week. Louise said yes and the following week she became part of the team at the Canyon, she was doing a job she loved.

When it was time for Luke to leave she was very disappointed, she had very much enjoyed working with him. He told her that the week of lectures had been the best he had ever done. He made her promise to keep in touch and said he would try and get back in the spring, and maybe they could hike down into the Canyon.

Louise was very popular with the visitors and she became better each day at her job as she relaxed into it and learned more about the Canyon from others.

One day she was asked if she would like to go into the Canyon on a hike with some tourists, she of course said yes, it was a group of twelve tourists' eight men and four women. It was a nice group apart from one man who thought he was an expert on everything, he would not listen to any of the safety briefings and every time someone advised him on something he deliberately did the opposite he was a regular Mr know it all, and although his name was Dan he soon earned the name "Dumb Ass Dan" because he liked to do things his way. Basically he was an idiot.

The hike was for five days and by the last day everyone had had more than enough of Dumb Ass Dan and tempers were starting to fray. He had been rude to the women and very derogatory causing some near punch ups with the other men and causing the rangers to intervene on a few occasions.

They set up camp and settled down for their last Canyon night. The Rangers were telling their stories as usual, Dumb Ass Dan was sitting at the front and sniggering at everything they said questioning their integrity and knowledge. One of the Rangers, Paul, asked Louise if she would like to tell them about her upbringing at the Canyon and how her family had earned a living.

She jumped at the chance and stood in front of the group, she smiled sweetly at everyone and as usual they were enchanted by her smile, beautiful blue eyes and dark hair. The women loved her and were fascinated by her childhood. She told them how she had educated herself and how her and her mother baked cakes and biscuits to earn a living.

At this point Dumb Ass Dan decided he wanted to ask her a question. She smiled at him and welcomed his question.

"Do you have a professional qualification in guiding us or are you here to sell your cakes little lady, isn't there a kitchen somewhere missing its bitch" he said

All of the women gasped and looked at him with disgust, Paul stepped up to Louise to relieve her of having to answer such a disgusting question, but she stood her ground.

"How long are you staying at the Canyon for Sir" she asked

"Oh about three weeks till I get bored" he replied sniggering.

"Well" said Louise, "Feel free to leave whenever you please, we would hate to deprive a village of its idiot for too long"

The camp went silent and for once so did Dumb Ass Dan.

She then said to him

"I have found your attitude on the hike extremely selfish and monopolising and if you don't shut the hell up I will have you lifted out of the Canyon and dumped on the North Rim in desolate House Rock Valley"

He stood up and looked her in the face he was red with anger, but she stood her ground, Paul and another Ranger Gary stood up but did not interfere she had given them a look which warned them not to.

"It may be news to you little lady but the Canyon is not owned by you, it's for everyone so you can't have me lifted outta here I am a free man and I can go and do as I god dammed please" he said

"Yes sir" she replied "You are completely right so why don't you stop complaining you may actually enjoy yourself" Thinking he had won the battle he sat down looking smug next to the fire smirking to himself.

Louise sat away from the fire and brought out a bottle from her bag, she made a point of being covert with it and this of course caught Dumb Ass Dan's attention. He stood up and complained in front of everyone that she was drinking something alone and had not offered to share; he said that everything should be shared out equally. Louise apologised to him and told him he was right, she handed him the bottle and invited him to help himself but to please pour it into a mug and not drink it from the bottle.

Everyone else looked on but she gave them a smile which they all read to be a wise one and said they didn't want any.

He poured out half a mug and knocked it back in one. Gary and Paul looked on they knew what it was, it was moonshine, and they knew she could get into trouble for having it but neither of them were going to say anything to anyone.

Ma cahu

They sat around the fire and told some more stories. One of the women asked Louise if she had a man in her life but Louise said she had not found one just yet. The lady told her that a beautiful girl like her would find the right man one day and probably when she was not even looking for him.

Dumb Ass Dan piped up again

"Yea then you can get back to a kitchen and do the job you were born to do" he threw his head back in laughter, by this time he had drunk half a bottle of moonshine and when he threw his head back he lost his balance and fell backwards, he tried to stop himself but ended up flat on his back. He tried to move his legs into a position to help himself up but unfortunately he had developed the moonshine spaghetti legs and couldn't move.

He lay there and slept. What a result! Now the rest of the group could enjoy the evening in peace.

The next morning they woke ready for their hike out of the Canyon they were all refreshed after a good sleep and although sad to leave they were looking forward to the beautiful scenery on the way out and a comfy bed at the end of the evening.

Dumb Ass Dan was not too good however, he had a hangover from hell and was suffering badly, no one had any sympathy for him, just gave him plenty of water and told him to carry on and not let the group down. He blamed Louise, saying she gave him some sort of poisonous drink and she should be fired from her job. He went on and on about it and said

"I am going to put in a complaint about that bitch when I get to the rim"

By this time Ranger Gary had enough, he told him to shut up but Dumb Ass kept going on and on, eventually Gary stopped the group and said

"Shut the hell up, you have ruined the experience of a lot of people over the last few days and made my job and the job of my colleagues a nightmare. You complained Louise was not sharing her bottle of water with you so she did share it, now you accuse her of poisoning you, if you say one more word I will personally see to it that you are fined for violations you committed during your hike into the Canyon"

"I broke no violations" he replied

Gary looked at him and said

"Oh yes you did you left your litter on the ground, you fed the wildlife and you took a bottle of bootleg moonshine in there with you,"

He opened his mouth to speak, to defend himself against the accusations which were fictitious, but the whole of the group looked at him and smiled.

"Yes" said Gary we have quite a few witnesses don't we, now get your fat arse up that trail and shut the hell up"

Everyone in the group was trying not to laugh and had to turn their heads away. Dumb Ass Dan had finally been shut up and sulked for the rest of the trip.

From that day on Louise became stronger in personality her job and the variety of people she met, along with some of the things she saw, helped to shape her as a person and helped her to see life in a different way, she was no longer as naive and had become tougher and much wiser.

Dumb Ass Dan was not the only idiot of his type she met there were plenty more where he came from, but she handled each situation brilliantly and was admired by everyone she worked with for her fairness, kindness, but no messing attitude. Every weekend she returned home to her mother and brothers, her mother didn't have to bake so much now because Louise was bringing home a wage.

In the spring as promised Luke returned, he spent a week with her and they hiked a good part of the Canyon, he told her he wanted to stay at the Canyon for a while longer. She was pleased and said it would be nice for him to stay because there would be lots for him to study, he told her he wanted to stay because he had fallen in love with her and was hoping she would do the same if he was around for a while longer.

She confessed that she had been thinking about him a lot and would like to spend more time with him. They courted for a long time and were inseparable. Anne was very pleased she liked Luke a lot.

One weekend they returned home to the house and Anne told them that there had been a few deaths locally, someone had been distilling moonshine and had made red stuff. It was of great concern to the police and if they didn't find out who it was they were afraid the deaths would continue, folk were supposed to set it alight to see which colour it glowed. That Saturday afternoon I called to the house, I introduced myself as Skippity Jack Moran, I was passing to see the Sheriff about the moonshine problem and called in to buy some biscuits as I was hungry.

Anne made me some coffee and we got talking about the moonshine. I told her that the moonshine I distilled was made in a strictly controlled environment and I took it very seriously so I was going to advise the Sheriff about the recent problem. Anne was very interested and asked me if I had a sample, I did and gave it to her. She had a sip and thought it was very nice she had not tasted it before as she was not a drinker, but she enjoyed it. She asked me if I would teach her how to distil it. I was a bit reluctant because it was a secret recipe but we came to an agreement, I would give her the recipe and I would show her how to distil it but I would leave out one of the ingredients so she could add her own and have originality.

She told me I could have the biscuits and gave me some extra for my journey and for helping her. She said that if we made a safe moonshine and folk trusted us they would buy from us all the time and we would make money, the local moonshine drinkers would be safe, and it would also flush out the red distiller. I thought she was brilliant; she had a good head for making a profit and knowing how to use a situation to her advantage.

We set a day for me to teach her and I brought the stuff she needed. We both went to Sheriff Earl and told him of our idea, by this time there had been more deaths and it was getting out of control, he agreed to a trial period to see if it would bring the amount of deaths down. He was doing it without authorisation and could get into serious trouble but at this stage anything was worth a try. It was clear by the amount of deaths how many people were drinking moonshine anyway, so it was a problem which was already out of control. Sheriff Earl visited everyone he suspected may be drinking any sort of moonshine from any source and told them where to get the safe stuff from. We were in business, and within a few weeks the death rate dropped dramatically.

We continued to supply the local area, but we couldn't mark the bottles to say where they came from and everyone had to come to one of us for it. We never sold more than two bottles at a time and we never sold in bulk to someone who could sell it on. We were very strict.

We became very good friends and I spent a lot of time with her, every weekend when Louise came home she also learned the distilling process so she could help when there was a high demand. Eventually the deaths stopped and we were told to carry on, it was obviously doing good so we continued producing it.

One evening, I arrived at the house to bring some of my moonshine, it was very quiet, I knocked on the door and Anne answered, she fell into my arms sobbing, Louise and Luke had been in the Canyon, when they sat down for a coffee and a rest, they heard someone shouting

"Rock"

Louise and Luke Jumped up, but he tripped over and fell, Louise ran to him and tried to drag him out of the way but his foot was caught, she managed to release it and helped him to his feet, they ran towards the Canyon wall to take shelter under a ledge, but the rock had caused more unsettlement and another rock hit Luke hard on the side of his head. Louise did what she could and help did get to him but it was too late, he had suffered a massive trauma to his head and he had no chance of survival. Louise sat with him cradling him in her arms, she told him he had to go on because she was expecting a baby and he was going to be a father, he smiled at her and his eyes shone with tears of joy, she kissed his forehead and as she did he died in her arms.

She had been taken to the hospital to be checked over and was now in bed; she was traumatised beyond belief and had been given something to help her sleep.

After that day Louise never spoke of Luke again, she gave birth to their son six months later when she was just eighteen years old. She was a wonderful mother, kind and gentle. After a few years her brothers married and moved on and her mother to my own personal sadness died at the young age of forty five. So it was just her and her son Luke Junior, who was and still is a lovely person.

The son Luke had was adopted he had found him abandoned by the side of the road one day on his way to Flagstaff when he was just sixteen. He treated the child as his own son and became legal guardian of him, which was a very mature thing for a boy of his age to do.

The child was brought up by them both, Luke Junior went to work in Phoenix when he was twenty one, and Louise told him to take Michael with him because she believed he would have a better education there, but I know she missed him very much, she doted on the two boys. She started the baking business again and she had continued with the moonshine since her mother died anyway, so it brought the money in and kept her busy.

After a while she became accustomed to the moonshine, probably due to the amount of sampling she had to do, and could drink anyone under the table, it also loosened her tongue and brought out the worst of her, she never hurt anyone but she had the most interesting vocabulary and no one to this day knew where such a beautiful lady had learnt it from. I spent many a warm evening with her on the porch getting wasted on moonshine and sucking pickled eggs and plucking away on my banjo.

By the time she created you she had done a lot in her life time, she never loved again, but I always kept an eye on her and made sure she was alright. She was just forty four years old when she died and we lost a wonderful woman, a woman with true grit"

CHAPTER TWENTY-THREE

Willie and Spike set off early in the morning for their journey to Flagstaff train station they went by mule. Jane went with them so she could return with the mules. She was very sad to see Willie and Spike go but she knew they would be alright.

When they arrived at Flagstaff it was very busy it was getting cold and there was some light snow. They arrived at the train station and said their goodbyes. Willie and Jane hugged each other tightly and Jane gave Spike a good hug too. They boarded the train and set off for Sky Harbour Airport Phoenix.

Jane rode back to the house she decided she would start baking the next day because she needed to keep busy the house was very quiet and very lonely.

Spike absolutely loved the train he rode the whole way to Phoenix with his head sticking out of the window even though Willie advised him not to. As they moved towards Phoenix it did become a little warmer, Willie was very nervous, everything seemed so different he had never been anywhere bigger than Flagstaff.

When they were close to the station the guard came and told Spike to put his head back into the carriage or he may lose it because of the other trains using the station, Spike had seen Fanny's head separated from her body and didn't want the same thing to happen to his so did as he was told. While his head had been out of the window he had kept his face in the same position throughout the journey his tongue was out and he was panting, it looked like he had a permanent grin on his face and his ears were blown back.

When he brought his head back into the carriage his face didn't change, the muscles in his face and ears had seized in the cold air outside the window, he could move his tongue back and forth but not back into his mouth and he could move his eyes around, but nothing else. His face was frozen in position he looked like he was stood in front of a huge powerful fan.

Willie told him to stop messing about and put his face back to normal but he couldn't. When Willie realised this he was horrified, poor Spike had a paralysis to his face. The guard on the train passed them again and popped his head around the carriage door to make sure Spike didn't still have his head out of the window. The guard took one look at Spike and laughed so much Willie thought he would run out of air, when he eventually calmed down he told Spike that the problem should wear off after a couple of days, he saw it happening all the time with little kids but Spike's frozen expression was the best he had ever seen.

Willie and Spike got off the train and took a taxi to the airport, it looked as though Spikes head had been the stuffed by a taxidermist but his body hadn't. Willie found it very difficult to look at him without laughing. When they arrived at the airport there was a slight problem because although Willie didn't need a passport because he was technically a biscuit, Spike did need one and he had one, but the picture looked nothing like him. Although a known fact that no one's passport picture ever looks like them, Spike of course was at a bigger disadvantage.

The security guard called for a doctor to come and check Spike over, they took him into a private room and he was examined. The doctor confirmed he was who he was and explained it was a temporary problem. Free to go they sat in the departure lounge. Willie bought them food as they had not eaten all day and a coffee. Spike had to have a straw for his coffee and Willie had to put the straw filled with coffee down his throat and blow, he also had to do the same with his food.

People who saw this odd behaviour didn't sit near them for long and it was actually quite frustrating because Spike couldn't tell Willie what he wanted all he could do was make paw signals so Willie had to go through a list of things every time Spike wanted something. Eventually their flight was called and they made their way to the departure gate. Spike was feeling pretty pissed off by now and would have been down in the mouth if he had any control over it.

Willie said when they got onto the plane he would ask the stewardess if Spike could go into the cockpit with the pilots to cheer him up. Spike would have smiled if he had any control over his mouth. They settled into their seats and waited for the aircraft to take off, neither of them had flown before so had no idea what to expect. As the aircraft sped down the runway, they both looked out of the window, they could feel it lift into the air and it went higher and higher. Willie looked terrified and Spike would have too if he had any control over his face. The only good thing was that because he couldn't move his face his specs didn't keep falling over his nose and need to be pushed up every ten seconds.

The stewardess said that she had spoken to the captain and he said after their meal Willie and Spike would be most welcome to visit the cockpit. They were served their meals first because Willie explained Spikes predicament and that it took him twice as long to eat his food. When the food came Willie ate his quickly so it didn't get cold then he fed Spike through a straw again. He noticed that Spikes tongue was getting very dry because it was sticking out of his mouth so he wet it with some water. Spike showed is gratitude by moving his eyes from side to side.

The stewardess as promised came and invited them both to the cockpit once she had cleared up the meals. Willie was excited and assured them that Spike was too. She opened the door of the cockpit and they walked in.

"Welcome to the cock pit" said the pilot, he looked at Willie and smiled then he looked at Spike

"What the hell happened to your face dude looks like someone pressed the pause button" Spike would have been angry if he had any control over his face.

Both pilots burst into laughter. Willie was very cross it was a very unprofessional way to speak to a paying passenger. The pilot could see Willie wasn't happy and apologised he gave them a massive bar of chocolate as a way of an apology and asked them if they wanted to sit in the pilot and co pilot seats.

Willie let Spike sit in the pilot's seat and he sat in the co pilot's seat. They were flying over the coast of America and until now they had no idea how big the world was. Willie had never seen the ocean for real and to see it for the first time by air was awesome as they flew along the coast towards Nova Scotia. Spike had seen the ocean when he had gone to the beach with his master once, they had taken a picnic, and he remembered that particular day clearly because he had been allowed to have butter on his bread as a treat. He would have told them of his day at the beach if he had any control over his mouth.

They loved it, looking out of the window from miles high was amazing they were very careful not to touch any buttons. The pilots introduced themselves as Spud and Duke, Duke was the main pilot. After half an hour Willie told Spike they had troubled the nice pilots for long enough and they should go back to their seat and get some sleep.

Duke and Spud told them to enjoy the rest of the flight and the food, Willie said the food they had already eaten was delicious and he looked forward to the next meal. He explained that he had to feed Spike but he loved every straw full as he had lived on bread and water all his life until Willie had met him because he had a cruel master. Willie then placed a small bottle of moonshine into each of the pilot's hands and gave them a wink. When they left the cockpit, Spud turned to Duke and said

"Poor bastard such a nice little dog too, but I have to say Willie must be one hell of a good friend for that little dog not to have eaten him yet, he smelt darn good didn't he"

Duke agreed and they continued to fly the plane.

Willie and Spike settled into their seats and after a short while drifted off into a welcome slumber until Spike was woken suddenly by being thrust forwards repeatedly in his seat which was very annoying. He sat up looked behind him and saw a little kid of about four years old kicking the back of his seat. He couldn't speak so he nudged Willie to wake him so he could ask the kid to stop. Willie was so unconscious with sleep that he was dribbling out of the corner of his mouth Spike knew he had no chance of waking him.

He thought that if he lay his seat back a little the kid would not be able to kick it and he would be more comfortable too, he was wrong, the little mutant still kept kicking his seat. What annoyed Spike even more was that the kid's mother was sleeping peacefully right next to him and was oblivious to what her little brat of a kid was doing.

As the kicking continued Spike became more and more agitated, he had no way of calling for assistance so he did the only thing he could do in the situation, he turned around again and starred at the little kid as piercing as his eyes would let him, his specs magnifying them massively. Spike hoped his funny face would stop the kid from kicking his chair but it didn't the kids face turned white and he let out the loudest scream Spike had ever heard. The kid jumped up on his seat and cried, tears running down his face, his mother didn't move she was still asleep probably because there were at least ten empty miniature bottles of brandy on the tray in front of her.

Willie did wake at this point he looked behind him to see the little kid in a state of hysteria, Spike not being able to tell Willie what had happened, tried to act out the scene to Willie and in doing so kicked the seat of the person in front of him, the woman occupying the seat turned around and slapped Spike across his face. His face could not feel the pain, but she had a dangly bracelet on which whipped around his neck and slapped a sensitive spot on his back. It hurt so much that Spike would have cried if his face would have allowed him to, instead tears rolled down his little face and steamed up his specs.

The stewardess who had taken them to the cockpit came over to see what all the fuss was about. She gave the kid a chocolate bar to shut him up as his mother was obviously incapable of doing the job. She asked the woman why she had slapped Spike, and she said he had been kicking her seat. Spike couldn't answer for himself just sat still while tears continued to fall down his face.

The woman was horrible she stood up and demanded that she be moved to first class away from the freaky looking mutt and the oversized biscuit. She said she was far too superior to be sat with the likes of them. The stewardess was not stupid she met her type on every shift. She told the woman she would shuffle things around, if she would like to go to the bathroom and calm down for a moment, when she returned things would be sorted out. The woman tried to hide the look of smug satisfaction on her face as she strutted off to the bathroom.

Willie apologised to the stewardess he tried to explain what had happened but she told him and Spike to collect their belongings and leave their seats. Willie knew they were in trouble now he and Spike followed the stewardess towards the cockpit this time they would be going in there for a good telling off from Spud or Duke.

They were wrong. She led them to another part of the plane and sat them in different seats. Wow they were in first class. A few moments later they could hear the bitch who had been sitting in front of Spike yelling at the stewardess, she was then told by the captain that she would be arrested if she didn't sit down and shut up.

Willie and Butt had a wonderful time for the rest of the trip, they were served strawberries and champagne and as much cake as they could eat, of course Spike's had to be fed via the straw method but he still enjoyed it especially as drinking champagne that way restricted the oxygen to his brain enabling him to get off his face quicker. They were served chocolates, fruit and coffee on the hour every hour. Soon they were completely stuffed and fell asleep while watching the in flight movie. What a result.

After a five hour flight they landed at Halifax Airport they were escorted off the aircraft by a lovely lady named Jessica and taken to collect their luggage, they didn't have much just one small bag between them. Spike didn't need clothes and Willie just had one outfit identical to the one he was wearing and some spare underpants. Jessica also sorted out the passport problem Spike had because again passport control didn't recognise him.

They waited patiently for their bag to come through, Willie was very tired and just wanted to go to sleep. Opposite them a small child was holding a rabbit soft toy Willie was amazed at how realistic it looked. The kid obviously loved it because it was holding on to it tightly. Suddenly the baggage carousel started to move and made a loud noise, the little kid jumped and dropped its rabbit onto the carousel none of the baggage had been placed on it yet and the rabbit started to go around much to the distress of the child.

Spike's attention was immediately caught and he jumped onto the carousel he couldn't help it, it was instinct. The kid was crying, Spike was running and the rabbit was going around and around. Spike was slowly gaining on the fluffy toy and as he tackled the corners Willie was impressed at how agile he was. The problem was, Spike couldn't turn his frozen head so when he turned the corners, his body went with the flow but his head didn't.

There were a three teenage boys waiting for their baggage they saw Spike and could not stop laughing, Willie shouted at Spike to get off the carousel at once but Spike was on a mission he was going to catch that rabbit no matter what.

Suddenly one of the idiot teenagers thought it would be a laugh to jump on with Spike and chase him around, he jumped on but landed in front of Spike not behind him and his friends cheered him on. The father of the little kid was furious he tried to grab the rabbit every time it went past but missed he also tried to grab Spike but missed him too.

Unfortunately the baggage was released onto the carousel just as the stupid teenager was passing the loading point, he tried to stop himself from running but tripped over his loose shoe laces which he had been too lazy to tie up and landed flat on his face. Everyone started to laugh and he disappeared under the rubber flaps followed by Spike.

Willie was furious when Spike emerged from the other end of the rubber flaps again he demanded he came off the carousel immediately, Spike ignored him. Strangely there was no sign of the teenager he should have come out before Spike.

As the rabbit went around another corner, Spike launched himself off the one side and onto the other cutting the corner so he could get the rabbit, he caught it in his front paws. By this time a security guard had seen what was happening and pressed the emergency stop button the carousel came to a sudden halt Spike flew off clutching the toy rabbit and landed in the lap of the woman who had been in the seat in front of him on the aeroplane, her coffee spilt all over her designer suit, she picked Spike up and threw him he landed hard on the floor and yelped out in pain.

Everyone at the carousel turned and looked at the woman, Spike was crumpled on the floor, he would have shown the pain he was in if he could have moved his face. Although in agony, Spike dragged his little body over to the little kid pushing the rabbit along with his chest and gestured to the child with his paws to take the toy.

Everyone was moved at Spikes actions, they like Willie thought he was just feeding his natural instinct but no, he was saving the child's fluffy rabbit. The woman from the aeroplane was still ranting about her suit but no one took any notice of her they just looked at Spike.

A lady went up to Spike and had a look at him, she felt his little body. She couldn't feel any broken bones but thought he may be very bruised so she picked him gently and carried him to a seat putting him down carefully. Their bag had arrived and Willie grabbed it and took it over to where Spike was.

Willie realised at that point that he had not made any travel arrangements for them and they were both very tired. The father of the baby with the stuffed rabbit came over and introduced himself as Andy, he said he was very sorry Spike had been hurt while retrieving the toy and asked them where they were heading. Willie told him they were going to visit a lady near St Mary's river. Andy said he could take them as far as Truro if that helped, and showed Willie a map.

Willie accepted the ride. Andy said they could sleep in the car on the way it wouldn't take long, but at least they would have some rest. When they got outside it was freezing. They hadn't brought any warm clothes with them and although the Canyon did get cold in winter, when they had left it was mild compared to Nova Scotia. Andy went into a bag and took out two thick warm jumpers belonging to his little boy and gave them one each, they were lovely and cosy. They climbed into the car.

Andy said he was on his way home, he and his son had been to see his mother in Phoenix and his wife had stayed home because she could not stand his mother and wouldn't stay in the same room as her.

Wille didn't hear any more of the conversation because he fell asleep, and so did Spike.

An hour later, Andy woke them to tell them he had taken them as far as he could go. He pointed them in the right direction towards a lonely looking road and said they had to follow that road until they found the house they were looking for. They thanked Andy and waved goodbye.

It was late afternoon and they still had a good few hours day light to get to Eve's house. As they walked along it started to snow.

CHAPTER TWENTY-FOUR

They set off along the road which Andy had told them to follow, Willie said it twisted and turned just like the Colorado River. When they had been walking for a couple of hours, they were very tired. The temperature was dropping again and it was still snowing.

Luckily they soon came across a lay by and in the lay by was a truck which was loaded up with logs. Willie decided they should get on the truck and see how far it would take them towards their destination. When they saw the signs for St Mary's River they would get off the truck and look for Eve's house which was called "Blueberry"

They climbed aboard the truck and found a gap between the side of the truck and the logs to keep out of the wind. Not long after they had climbed aboard and settled down they heard the engine of the truck start up, it moved slowly at first off the lay-by and onto the road where it continued at a steady pace.

They were very happy to have found a way of shortening their journey, they found a piece of rag in the back of the truck and used it to keep themselves warm and cuddled up together. As the truck bounced along the road and they were rocked back and forth by the motion Willie and Spike fell asleep.

They travelled for fifteen miles while they were sleeping and were woken by a jolt and for a moment were confused as to where they were. Suddenly Spike let out a massive fart and sat up. His nose could smell something, he was very excited, and it definitely was not his fart he could smell as he had become used to that aroma.

What he could smell was bacon, sausage and toast, he lifted his tail so he could balance himself on the side of the truck and lean over towards the smell of the food, this prompted Willie to dive for cover as he thought the lifting of the tail was a sign that another fart was on the way.

Spike started scratching at the logs to try and get Willie out from his hiding place to tell him about the food, but Willie was too afraid to come out in case he got it full in the face, but then as the stench of the fart gave way he too could smell food cooking. He lay there and relaxed breathing in the smell of the hot food; although they had not gone hungry the smell of the food was just too much to resist.

Soon he had been dug out by Spikes claws and as he looked up his furry pal was starring into his eyes Willie was relieved that he was looking at the end which had the two eyes.

Spikes little face would have been showing extreme excitement if he'd had any control over it. Willie sat up and wiped the slobber from his face which had dripped onto him from Spike, the smell of the food was making his mouth water and he had no control over the drooling. He looked out over the side of the truck to see if he could find where the smell was coming from. They had pulled into a big yard and there were lots of other trucks with logs on them too.

A group of men were gathered outside a door way, they were chatting and drinking from mugs. Willie realised that the men were standing outside a log cabin which was being used as a cafe. The door opened and the smell became even stronger, the men went inside.

"You know what Spike we could do with some of that food it would keep our bellies nice and warm" said Willie.

They jumped down from the back of the truck and made their way over to the cafe, Willie opened the door and they walked inside, the place fell silent and everyone turned to look at them. They walked over to a table and sat down, the waitress came over and Willie ordered two large all day breakfasts and two mugs of coffee.

Once they had ordered everyone else turned back to what they were doing and stopped staring at them.

Spike indicated to Willie that he needed to go outside for a pee, and off he went. While he was outside Spike couldn't help but have a good nose around. At the back of the cafe was an old spring mattress and above that was a window. Spike climbed up onto the mattress and started to bounce. As he gained momentum he jumped higher and higher, he wanted to see if he could see Willie inside and make him laugh.

The window looked directly into the cafe and was open slightly. Spike looked so funny as he bounced, his gums and lips flapped about and he made raspberry noises, his face was still frozen in expression but the very loose bits still had some independence, each time he came down, the strain of each jump prompted a small fart.

Eventually Spike was noticed by Willie as intended, but he had also captured the attention of the other diners. They wondered what the hell he was doing and so did Willie, one of the men started to laugh and started everyone else laughing the whole place was soon in fits of laughter. What a sight, a semi paralysed mutt jumping up and down at the window was just too much. Eventually, out of breath Spike stopped bouncing and came down off the mattress. He had a pee, walked back into the cafe and sat down to his breakfast.

He had been oblivious to everyone else watching him as he had focused on making Willie laugh, so when he saw a group of fat men rolling about laughing he thought he had missed something.

Willie told him to just sit still while he fired his food down his throat with a straw Spike sat opposite Willie and was fed. By the time the men had got up from the floor, Willie and Spike were half way through their food.

One of the men came over to them and introduced himself as Todd. Willie thought they were going to get told off but Todd said he and his friends had just had the best laugh and the best entertainment in a long time and thanked them. He asked Willie what had happened to Spikes face and Willie explained.

Todd walked outside to his truck, he searched around inside the cabin for a few minutes and then returned with a tub. He handed it to Willie and told him to rub it into Spikes face and within a couple of minutes his muscles would be relaxed and normal again. Willie finished feeding Spike, gave him his coffee and then finished his own food. Spike looked at the tub and his eyes looked inpatient so Willie opened the tub to massage the contents into Spikes face.

They were both almost thrown off their seats, the smell was terrible, Todd said that if it didn't smell bad then it wouldn't work so to rub it in and they would soon get accustomed to the stench. Willie took a big blob and spread it all over Spikes face and ears, his fur was wet and matted with the stuff and he looked terrible but if it worked they didn't care.

The waitress brought another two coffees on the house for them, the guy who gave them the cream said Spike should start to feel something by the time they had finished their coffee.

Sure enough Spike could feel something happening, it was just a slight tingling at first but that soon turned into a warm feeling, he was able to start moving his nose, he could wiggle it slightly and his ears started to fall into their normal position. Amazingly, by the time they had finished their coffee Spike had most of the feeling back in his face.

Willie thanked Todd, he was just pleased to help after the entertainment they had provided, he told them he used it all the time on his sheep who insisted on sticking their heads out of the truck on the way to the auction. Who the hell wanted to buy sheep with faces frozen in a grin.

Stuffed to the brim like a pair of turkeys they were ready for the next part of their journey it was starting to get dark and Willie wanted them to get to Eve's house before night fall. The lady at the cafe told them they were on the right track to "Blueberry" and they only had a few miles to go.

One of the other guys offered them a ride but Willie said they should walk off the huge breakfast they had eaten.

Spike was thrilled to have his face back, even if his specks did start to fall forward again, he was pulling all sorts of weird faces, sticking his tongue in and out and snapping his jaw shut and smacking his lips. This was funny at first but after an hour started to annoy Willie to the point where he wanted to slap him hard.

After a little while they came to a group of three houses all evenly spaced with beautiful gardens, Spike immediately went up to the first bush he could find and cocked his leg up against it, smiling as he did so. Willie was quite ashamed at his behaviour at times he really was. They looked at the name on the first house, it was called "Strawberry" The second house was "Blueberry" They had arrived at Eve's house there was a light on and it looked warm and cosy.

They were about to knock on the door when Willie had a thought, what if her gingerbread people had not come to life and she had eaten them, if she answered the door to Willie he may be the one who gives her a heart attack. All they wanted to know was that she was alright. Willie said he would hide behind a bush and Spike was to bark outside the front door then maybe Eve would come out to see what all the noise was about and they could see that she was alive and well.

Just as Spike was about to bark, the neighbour from "Strawberry" came out and went to Eve's house. She opened Eve's front door and called to her, Eve came to the door and the neighbour handed her a lovely looking cake. Eve thanked her and they said good night.

Well that was that, Eve was alive and well and there was no longer any need to worry about her. Willie noticed a telephone box across the road and said he was going to call Jane and tell her the good news.

When he called the house was very noisy there was a lot of laughter in the background. Jane told Willie that Luke Junior and Michael had made a surprise visit. Butt had arrived and Sheriff Earl was there too collecting some moonshine which Skippity Jack had left for him. Butt was entertaining them and little Michael was having a fantastic time with him.

It sounded so good and everyone was having so much fun, it made Willie feel very home sick. Jane was thrilled when he told her Eve was alive and kicking, and they had seen her with their own eyes. He put the receiver down and walked back to Eve's house, he wanted to take a peek into the window to take a look at Ma Cahill's good friend.

When he and Spike looked through the window he could see Eve, she was sat watching television and laughing, sitting next to her on the arm of the chair were three little gingerbreads, they were watching television and laughing too, she smiled at each of them and gave them a kiss. Willie took the letter Ma Cahill had written for Eve and put it in her mail box. He turned to Spike and said

"Come on Spike everything looks fine here let's go home to the Canyon"

Lightning Source UK Ltd.
Milton Keynes UK
UKOW050148251011

180885UK00004B/2/P